To Hunt a Sainte

Praise for Marie Harte's
To Hunt a Sainte

"Marie Harte pens a great tale that is in keeping with previous books that made me a fan. There's enough taste of paranormal with the mixed bag of psychic abilities to make this a unique tale. Sexy men and a strong woman who won't be run over by the macho, overprotective personalities around her, all make for a great story. There are plenty of erotic scenarios to tantalize and keep us interested. There's also those bits of tongue in cheek humor that always overlay Ms. Harte's work and make it fresh and fun."

~ *The Romance Studio*

"TO HUNT A SAINTE is a wonderfully written suspense thriller that had me sitting on the edge of my seat from the beginning to the end. ...Marie Harte pens a novel that will draw readers in with her charismatic characters and sexual tension that is hot enough to scorch your fingers as you are turning the pages."

~ *Romance Junkies*

Look for these titles by
Marie Harte

Now Available:

Cougar Falls Series
Rachel's Totem
In Plain Sight
Foxy Lady

Ethereal Foes Series
The Dragons' Demon
Duncan's Descent

Westlake Enterprises Series
To Hunt a Sainte
Storming His Heart

A Scorching Seduction
Enjoying the Show

Print Anthologies
Sins of Summer
I Dream of Dragons Vol. 1
Feral Attraction

To Hunt a Sainte

Marie Harte

SAMHAIN
PUBLISHING

Samhain Publishing, Ltd.
577 Mulberry Street, Suite 1520
Macon, GA 31201
www.samhainpublishing.com

To Hunt a Sainte
Copyright © 2011 by Marie Harte
Print ISBN: 978-1-60928-099-4
Digital ISBN: 978-1-60928-051-2

Cover by Kanaxa

First Samhain Publishing, Ltd. electronic publication: June 2010
First Samhain Publishing, Ltd. print publication: May 2011

Prologue

The warehouse stood apart from the rest of the run-down buildings on the wharf. One side of the building appeared brand new, the windows and doors polished and set as if constructed yesterday. The rest of the structure appeared as if out of a war zone, with large chunks of concrete and shards of glass strewn about the side streets with the rest of the trash.

Vagrants and prostitutes lined the outlying streets, giving subtle character to the aging monstrosity. The only saving grace the warehouse possessed was its view of the waterfront. On a clear day, sunlight glistened off the Savannah River, and sailboats and small motor craft raced through the water.

This particular evening, clouds blanketed the blue-gray sky. The trees whistled and whispered, the leaves seemingly turning from a dark green to a dull brown as the wind punished them ceaselessly. The scarred parking lot adjacent to the warehouse lay mostly empty, save for a few scattered and run-down cars.

A sharp glance at his watch showed the hour had reached eleven o'clock. Sweat trickled down his back, saturating his black cotton jacket. Even in September, Savannah possessed the ability to drain both energy and stamina from the most trained of men. Hunter Greye was no exception.

He willed his body to relax, to blend in with the

environment. Opening his senses, he listened to the alien silence, looked through the lingering blackness, and tasted the tang in the moist air. His gaze narrowed. Right...*there.*

At the northwest corner of the building, a security light had conveniently burned out. Dark shadows flitted through the night. Attuned to his environment, Hunter watched as two figures suddenly disappeared into a masked doorway, a hidden stairwell on the side of the building.

With a preternatural burst of speed, he cut across the parking lot and followed the intruders inside. In the stairwell, he stilled, listened for movement, and followed the faint noise above him.

Interesting that they bypassed security. Hunter kept close to the walls as he climbed the stairwell, careful to keep his image on the periphery of the cameras he hadn't disabled. Though the outside of the building projected a familiar air of helplessness and poverty, the inside boasted quite the opposite. Brick crumbled, but the mini-cam security system had been installed by the very best in the business—an unknown subsidiary of Westlake Enterprises, his employer.

He exited on the fourth floor, instinct guiding him toward Peter Omaney's office. Hunter listened with a forbidding sense of unease. Another set of sounds came from the hallway behind him. He darted into a shadowed alcove while four of Omaney's thuggish guards advanced on his mystery quarry.

Despite the glass frame around the closed office door, Hunter needed more than perfect vision to see in the dim light. He took a moment to *focus,* and the office space brightened. High-quality leather furniture and expensive art decorated Omaney's space. Photographs of the slick businessman shaking hands with prominent politicians graced the burnt orange walls while a state-of-the-art computer whirred to life on Omaney's solid-oak desk. Where two masked figures waited.

The arrival of security stopped the intruders' hasty search. The door burst open, and the largest guard waved a gun at them. "What the hell do you two think you're doing? Get away from the damned computer, on your knees."

The guards surrounded them, obviously expecting the masked figures to stop whatever they hell they had planned and kneel on the floor. Clad in black from head to toe, only one of the prowlers looked big enough to successfully engage his opponents. The other was smaller in comparison, a slim figure huddled behind the bigger male. So it came as a surprise to watch the smaller man attack first, taking down the largest guard with a kick to his gun hand and a punch to his neck. The intruder's partner moved with an efficient grace. He looked as if he spared little more energy than needed to subdue the guards, working in tandem with his companion.

In minutes, all four of Omaney's sentries sprawled bruised and unconscious on the floor, their guns in a pile on a nearby chair. The intruders had yet to speak. The larger of the two hurried back to the computer desk and plugged in a thumb drive. He typed at the keyboard, then waited, glancing repeatedly at the clock on the wall. The smaller figure remained still, vigilant while he—*or was that she?*—watched the doorway.

Hunter had sensed something odd about the smaller male, and now that he concentrated, he could make out a woman's form under all that black. She had taken on her attackers with ease, dispatching them quickly. Her large partner had been equally skilled at hand-to-hand combat, and Hunter reevaluated his assessment of the pair, wondering exactly why they sought to invade Omaney's space. These weren't ordinary burglars.

Nor was Omaney an ordinary businessman. Due to new

evidence Hunter's team had unearthed a mere week ago, he had no doubt Peter Omaney was involved in their current case. But he didn't know where these prowlers fit into the equation. It had taken his agency time and exhausting effort to get even a whiff of Omaney's involvement. The philanthropic businessman was squeaky clean. But obviously someone else knew there was more to Omaney than met the eye.

What the hell had they copied? Hunter needed a bead on the computer, but knew he had little time. Though he'd kept out of the way of the security cameras, these two had activated the motion sensors in Omaney's office. Even now, others rushed to investigate the warehouse's silent alarm. He needed to get his ass out of here. Yet...how had these two known to come *here*, to this particular site? Omaney kept this place off the radar.

Unfortunately, nothing about the masked pair seemed familiar. *Running out of time.* He willed them to reveal some important detail as to their identity before he was forced to flee. Westlake Enterprises couldn't afford to be linked to this break-in, or they'd blow their case.

As if hearing his plea, the man behind the computer did something fairly strange and decidedly stupid. He removed a black glove and placed his hand directly over the keyboard, lightly stroking the keys with his fingertips.

A chill bristled Hunter's spine, even as he scented the faint trace of extrasensory miasma—a cloying aroma Hunter associated with anything remotely psychic in nature. *Holy shit. Jurek needs to know about this, pronto.*

The man placed his hand back in the glove, pulled out and pocketed the memory stick, and turned off the computer. His accomplice tossed him a spray bottle and rag and waited while he wiped the keyboard clean of prints.

Saying nothing, they moved together out the office door.

Hunter remained still, watching with great curiosity as they backtracked their way to the exit. They paused while the large man listened at the top of the stairs. He nodded and exited, swallowed by the darkness.

Who the hell were they? More importantly, who were they working for? Hunter needed to get J.D.'s ass out here right away to look at that computer.

He waited for the woman to follow her partner and took a second shock to his system. She turned and looked right at him. Even in the dim light, Hunter could see her gray-green irises. With grudging respect, he studied those eyes that slowly examined his form hidden in the shadows.

When he remained unmoving, the woman disappeared into the darkness. He allowed her a small lead before he followed, his curiosity growing in leaps and bounds while he burned to know the woman's identity. But, when he reached the ground level, he found the exit door stuck in place. Swearing under his breath, he wrestled with it until the frame cracked and the door swung open.

He pushed through and swept the perimeter. To his immense frustration, they had vanished.

Chapter One

Alexandra Sainte shook her head upside-down as she blew it dry, wishing her hair resembled golden silk instead of a dirty mop. So much for highlights giving her character. She whipped her head up, felt the blood rush from her brain, and swore. A knock at the front door distracted her.

"I'll be out in a minute," she yelled as it chimed open. "You're early," she called out to her brother. Fastening the sad mess of her hair into a ponytail, she finished dressing in tan slacks and a short-sleeved sweater and joined Cole in the kitchen.

Glancing at his watch and then at her, he shook his head. "You're never on time."

Ignoring him, she moved into the kitchen to grab a yogurt and thrust a cup of coffee at him. Cole, like most of the males of Buchanan blood, couldn't boil water without specific, step-by-step instructions. The one time she'd tasted his coffee had been enough to scar her for life.

"So, what exactly do you have to complain about? It's Friday," she grumbled around a spoonful of breakfast.

"I still can't believe I let you talk me into going to that warehouse Wednesday night. You could have been hurt," he repeated.

"Enough, Cole. We've talked this to death. I'm a grown

woman and I make my own choices." They'd been discussing this for two days. Frankly, she was sick of trying to defend her right to live her life as she chose.

Cole scowled at her. "Fine. Can we get a move on? You know how he gets when we're late." He gulped down his steaming coffee. The dark circles under his eyes concerned her. She had a feeling his upset had more to do with what he'd learned than what she'd done.

"What did you get off the keyboard, Cole?"

"Nothing."

She didn't have her brother's psychometric abilities, but from what she knew about Omaney, touching anything that slimeball encountered would probably give her nightmares. On the outside, he seemed like the perfect gentleman. But from what they'd been told, Omaney was anything but. She could only imagine what Cole had seen. After several days of pestering, he still wouldn't tell her.

Wednesday night had gone like clockwork. They'd been in and out of Omaney's office in less than half an hour. The anticipated security gave them no problem. The only fly in the ointment, as far as Alex could tell, had been the golden-eyed observer watching them from the shadows.

Thanks to her handy work with the stairwell door, he hadn't followed them. Always careful, they hadn't left any identifiable clues or prints at the scene and had worn masks. Still, that observer bothered Alex on a number of levels. Not wanting to alarm Cole, she hadn't mentioned him. And if she tried really hard, she could almost forget the odd trembling she'd felt seeing those eyes fixed on her. Could ignore the way her heart had raced and her body had raged in uncontrollable, unexplainable lust the past two nights after dreaming about him.

15

Oh yeah, nothing to worry about. Just leftover adrenaline from the job mixed with a pathetic, nonexistent social life. That's all it is.

After finishing her breakfast, she poured herself a cup of coffee and then followed her brother out to his car. They arrived at work early for a change, easing her brother's foul mood.

"You rushed me for nothing. We're early. I hate being early," Alex muttered on the way up the elevator to her uncle's office.

Cole shrugged. "Yeah, well, I hate Uncle Max when he nags. And 'Late again?' is wearing thin. Besides, it's not as if you'd use the time to pretty yourself up." He sneered at her, as irritated with early mornings as Alex. "Try a little makeup, why don't you? No wonder you're perpetually dateless." They both knew she didn't hurt for male companionship when she wanted it. Alex, like her brother, had been blessed with good genes.

Giving her brother the argument he wanted, she followed him off the elevator, and they bickered down the long hallway toward their uncle's suite.

"Just because I'm choosey about who I date doesn't mean I can't get one," Alex said as they walked through the door to Max's outer office. "You nail anything in a skirt."

Cole snorted. "Please. I've never nailed a woman. I wine, I dine. I can't help it if they love me. I'm pretty, Alex. Just ask Christine."

Alex waited for Christine to join in the long-standing joke when she caught the cautious look on the secretary's face. Christine Harris had been with Max since the start of Buchanan Investigations over twenty years ago. She was calm in a crisis and withstood Max's odd moods without fault. Without her, Alex feared the firm would crumble.

That worried gleam in her ice blue eyes meant trouble.

Christine motioned them toward her. At the same time, Alex noted her uncle's closed door. Max rarely closed his door from Christine. The few times he had boded trouble.

"Jurek Westlake is in there with two dangerous-looking men," Christine whispered.

Alex stared wide-eyed at Christine before glancing at her brother, not surprised at his apparent shock. Before either of them could voice an opinion about Max's guests, his door opened.

"I need you two in here, now." Max glared and moved back from the doorframe, waiting.

Alex followed her brother, immediately seeking the enigmatic Jurek Westlake. A legend in the security business, he had a dangerous reputation that, according to Max, he'd earned. Roughly the same age as her uncle, like Max, he wore his years well. Close-cropped gray hair framed a masculine face full of arrogance and appraisal as he studied her and her brother with undisguised interest.

She shifted her glance to the men flanking him and did a double take. She knew those golden eyes, had seen them two days ago and each night since in her dreams...

"That's it, baby. Open for me," he murmured as he pushed her legs apart and slowly entered her. The heat, the stretching fullness, and the sense of union brought her close to begging for more. So attuned to her lover, she clutched him tight for a kiss and was rewarded when he began taking her in earnest. Thrusting in and out, harder and deeper. He angled himself so that every push grazed her clit, and before she could say his name, she seized in an explosive climax just as he tensed and spilled inside her.

She blinked to shake free of last night's dream and prayed her inner shields held her thoughts at bay. To her relief, her uncle, the mind reader, remained focused on Jurek.

The tall, dark stranger on Jurek's right was just as intense face to face as he was in her dreams—where he'd taken her again and again in ways that made her want to blush. He'd commanded her, body and soul, demanding everything while he fought through her defenses. In person, she could readily believe him capable of the same. The gleam in his gaze warned her to tread warily, because he looked as if he wanted to throw her over the couch and to hell with everyone else present.

Her brother took a step closer to her. "Alex?" he asked in a low voice.

Praying her sweater hid the effect the stranger was having on her body, she folded her arms over her chest and tore her gaze away. The tall blond on Jurek's left sat on Max's overstuffed sofa, oblivious to the strain in the room.

"Please, Jurek, Hunter, sit down." Max motioned to the couch, then frowned at Hunter, who had yet to look away from her.

Hunter finally blinked and, like a large cat, padded to the couch and sat gracefully next to the man already seated. Jurek sat on the other side, caging the blond between them.

Max waited for Alex and Cole to join him in the seats facing the couch. Together, the six of them sat in a large circle, staring at each other. Alex could literally feel the energy thrumming between them. The enemy, as she likened the men of Westlake Enterprises, resonated power.

Jurek Westlake owned and operated the rival investigative firm. Whereas Buchanan Investigations catered to private, discreet clients, Westlake's firm often worked high-profile cases and did occasional government work.

Alex found it telling that Jurek's people could get away with just about murder, cutting through legal red tape with ease,

18

whereas Buchanan Investigations had to move creatively, dancing around the fringes of legal propriety. Max didn't have the government connections that Westlake did, nor did he want them, as he'd said on more than one occasion.

She didn't know details, but her uncle had at one time worked for Uncle Sam. "I know better than to trust Big Brother," he was fond of saying.

"I'm sure we're all curious to know what exactly you're doing here before eight o'clock on a Friday morning," Max said pleasantly, his deep voice soothing while he verbally nudged Westlake for answers. "But please, forgive my manners. My nephew and niece, Cole and Alexandra Sainte."

Westlake grinned, charisma fairly oozing out of the snake charmer. *No wonder he gets so many clients. Hell, I'd do anything to keep him smiling. And that's damned weird.*

"Pleased to meet you both," Jurek said in an equally pleasant voice. "I'm Jurek Westlake. These are two of my finest men. J.D. Morgan." He pointed to the handsome blond sitting closest to him on the couch. "And Hunter Greye," he added, nodding at her mystery man with the predatory eyes.

Hunter certainly fit. He had yet to project an air of calm. Even sitting, he seemed dangerous, as if poised to spring at a moment's notice. Though he lounged indolently on the luxurious couch, he had an air of stillness about him at odds with his lazy grace.

"You two look familiar," he murmured, his gaze shifting from Cole to Alex, and lingering. His voice settled over her with uncomfortable appeal, and she fought the urge to squirm in her chair.

What the hell is wrong with me? Irritated by her strange reaction, Alex frowned. "Wish I could say the same," she muttered. By the look on Hunter's face, he was anything but fooled.

Max cleared his throat, drawing everyone's attention. "Let's quit screwing around. You're here for a reason, and we've all got better things to do than play twenty questions."

Jurek chuckled. "You know, Max, it's funny we haven't personally crossed paths before now. It's been what, ten years?"

"What do you want, Jurek?" Max asked again. He stared at Westlake in silence.

Alex could feel the power struggle through the tense air.

"Damn, Max, you've still got it," Westlake rasped.

She exchanged a glance with her brother. Could Westlake have been testing her uncle in *that* way? Her skin tingled, and she turned to find Hunter focused on her. His gaze didn't soften or stray from her face. He stared fixatedly at her eyes.

Alex felt a curious weakening in the pit of her stomach and an almost overwhelming urge to escape the room. Cole rested a protective hand on her shoulder, and his touch jolted her to break eye contact, concentrating on Westlake and her uncle once more.

Westlake sighed. "Fine, Max. I'll get right down to it. We believe one or two of your folks may have intruded on a case we're currently working. Wednesday night, one of our men saw two figures break into a private warehouse."

"A burglary? Why not call the police? They're friends of yours, aren't they?" Max asked pointedly.

"Let's just say this particular warehouse has been under our surveillance for a while. If we inform the police of our suspicions, we risk exposure and the possibility of tipping off our target."

"Who's your target?" Cole interrupted.

"Yes, who?" Max seconded.

"That's confidential information," Westlake answered. "Suffice it to say that anything obtained in that warehouse was done so illegally, and that in doing so you might be interfering in a government matter. We all know how much Buchanan Investigations dislikes doing business with Uncle Sam."

"Not so, Jurek." Max paused. "We just don't like the back-stabbing bureaucrats and candy-assed politicians more concerned with making a name for themselves than protecting the innocent."

"Amen," J.D. Morgan muttered.

Westlake scowled at him, and Alex watched in amusement as J.D. nudged Hunter with an elbow to the ribs and rolled his eyes. Apparently, Westlake's men had a bit of irreverence in them.

She studied J.D., noting the differences between him and Hunter. J.D. had model good looks—blond hair, bright blue eyes, and the high cheekbones and sharp features of a Scandinavian ancestor.

Hunter, on the other hand, looked like a tomcat dragged in off the street. Where his partner looked like he'd just stepped off the cover of *GQ*, Hunter looked like a suspect off *America's Most Wanted*. His dark hair and the hint of shadow along his jaw only added to his menacing air. Though he sat quietly, Alex could almost feel his impatience and frustration for some answers.

"Right, Alex?" Max said again. *"Get your head together, girl,"* he whispered in her mind.

"Right, Max." She had no idea to what she'd just agreed. She ignored her brother's pointed stare and tried to follow the conversation.

"So you see, Jurek, there's no way my people could have been in that warehouse Wednesday night," Max repeated. "Tell me whose warehouse it was. What exactly was taken?"

"I should have known better." Westlake shook his head, surprising Alex when he gave Max a sincere smile. Even more disturbing, her uncle returned the grin, looking happier than he had in months.

She knew her uncle and Westlake had a history, but she hadn't thought them amicable.

"Damn, but it was a good excuse to see you." Westlake and his men stood. "I'll look forward to our future run-ins."

"As will I." Max met him at the door and held out his hand.

They shook, then Westlake and J.D. filed out. Hunter paused next to Alex's chair.

She didn't want to look, but refused to take the easy way out. She deliberately met his gaze. *A mistake.* His eyes gleamed like gold, capturing her with his intensity.

"I'll be watching for you," he murmured. He nodded to both Cole and Max. When Westlake called after him, he left without looking back.

As soon as Hunter left the office, Max breathed a sigh of relief. "Damn. Those are some powerful people." He rubbed his temples and yelled for Christine.

"Max?" She appeared in the doorway as if she'd been waiting for his call.

"Would you mind grabbing us some coffee and the files on Mitchell?" he asked Christine. She nodded and left. Alex and her brother exchanged a knowing glance.

"What?" Max grumbled, any softness gone as he stared in vexation at his family. "Now, maybe you'd like to explain what *the hell* you were doing in Omaney's warehouse Wednesday night?"

There would be no getting around this one. Not with Westlake's men also involved. Alex resigned herself to an unpleasant lecture. "Well, you see, Cole accidentally touched the lipstick from Rebecca's purse—"

"Accidentally? You mean you *accidentally* took a piece of hard evidence from the police station?" Max's voice rose. "What's the matter with you two? Didn't you think there was a good reason I hadn't handed you anything of Rebecca's before now, Cole?"

Cole hung his head. Even at thirty, he couldn't escape his uncle's wrath, which amused Alex to no end.

"And you." Max glared at Alex. "I know you put him up to this."

No matter that Alex remained the younger sister by three years, or that no one forced her brother to do anything he didn't want to. Somehow, she'd garnered the reputation as the troublemaker in the family. Though, to be fair, taking the lipstick had been her idea.

"Yes, but—"

"No buts. Alex, you work in the office, not out in the field. Gathering information, doing research. I won't have you risking your neck when you're not ready for this kind of work."

"Uncle Max, I can do it."

"You haven't been trained."

And I never will be, not with you and Cole constantly mothering me.

Max continued to rant. "I knew Omaney had some involvement in Rebecca's disappearance. Hell, don't you think I do some work around here besides ordering everyone around?"

Christine entered with their coffees and three folders, giving Cole and Alex a moment's peace. But Max started in on them

23

the moment she left the office.

"Now, where were we?" he asked after a large sip of coffee.

"It's my fault." Cole spoke quickly to fend off another attack. Always her protector, her brother strove to intercede. As usual, his protection irritated her.

"No. It's *my* fault." Alex turned to Max. "I know Mrs. Mitchell came to see you Tuesday. I overheard her mention Rebecca's disappearance before she left your office. I just thought that if we could get a jump on Rebecca's past whereabouts, it could only help matters."

Grabbing the lipstick from the police station had been easy. A little flirting, a bit of telekinesis, some slight of hand, and she'd pocketed Rebecca's lipstick without touching it once. Once in Cole's hands, they'd learned about Peter Omaney. And after some more digging—and her cousin Luc's help—they'd found out about his dirty little warehouse.

"'Only help matters?'" Max repeated. He swore, but as he stared at her, his ire faded. "This is partially my fault for trying to keep a secret from you two."

Cole agreed. "You know keeping secrets around here is damned near impossible."

"Yes, well, for a bunch of psychics, we don't seem to be doing very well. Regardless of the danger, the reason I didn't want you checking on Peter Omaney is that he's been under Westlake surveillance for a good while."

"Damn." Alex shared a guilty look with her brother. "Then I guess it's a good thing we wore masks. They can't prove we were there."

"I'm afraid they will be able to." Max ran a hand through his hair. "While Rebecca's mother wants us to look into her disappearance, her father, the head of Mitchell Dynamics— which just happens to hold several large, government contracts—has contracted Westlake Enterprises for help. Boys and girls, we're not the only psychics working this case anymore."

Over steepled fingers, Jurek Westlake tracked the wild creature pacing in front of his desk and pondered Hunter's intensity. No longer having to put up a calm front in front of Max and his people, his agent reverted to form as he tried to contain that raging energy.

Hunter was large of frame and sound of mind. His predatory instincts made him a natural fit for Jurek's private security firm. A successful operation from its inception, Westlake Enterprises hired only the brightest and the best. Since hiring those men and women fell to him, Jurek naturally felt great confidence in the firm's ability to succeed.

But as he watched one of his most dangerous field agents pace in front of him, Jurek started to wonder if he'd have to keep a closer eye on his people. "Hunter, would you sit down? You're making me dizzy."

"You know they were lying through their teeth, don't you?" Hunter asked in a hard voice. Everything about him was hard, from his muscular frame to his rough hands to his granite-like face.

Jurek didn't answer.

Hunter huffed and threw himself into a chair on the other side of the desk. "So, what did they download from Omaney's computer?" he asked, just as J.D., their resident computer whiz, entered the office unannounced with the answer.

He sat next to Hunter, who regarded him with frustration. As usual, J.D. ignored him. "From the information Hunter brought me, I pieced together what little we already had on

25

Omaney with what our thieves copied. After a quick look at that hard drive, I noticed activity in two large folders labeled *Hotels* and *Properties*. Considering much of Omaney's fortune stems from his real estate ventures, those files shouldn't have run a red flag. However, the security on those particular folders exceeds everything else on his computer, including his finances."

"And?" Hunter prodded.

J.D. eyed him warily and continued. "*And*, after some scrutiny, some outstanding research, and brilliant deduction, I found a list of hotels he's recently visited that match with the last seven reported disappearances, of which Rebecca Mitchell happens to be one."

Jurek nodded. "Good work, J.D., Hunter. As you've no doubt realized, Max's folks are working this case. Rebecca disappeared Monday night. Harlan reported her missing Tuesday, when we took the case. This is definitely tied to the other missing women. No one witnessed Rebecca's disappearance."

"No one ever sees anything," J.D. grumbled.

"So how does Buchanan tie in to this?" Hunter frowned. "We only got wind of Mitchell's daughter recently. It's not in the papers. No one outside our agency or the Bureau's task force has tied Mitchell's daughter to the other disappearances over the past month."

"Harlan trusts us, but his wife decided to use the help of an old school friend—her old flame, Max Buchanan."

J.D. whistled. "Great. Now we're running a concurrent case with a bunch of amateurs. Granted, they have a reputation of getting the job done, but half the things they do border on being just this side of legal. You know that, don't you? They could make a real mess of this case. What do you want us to do? Take 'em out?"

Hunter snorted. "'Take 'em out?' How would you plan to do that? With a keystroke, maybe?"

While his agents traded barbs, Jurek firmed his decision. Time to turn this odd glitch into an opportunity. "J.D., I want you to stay on top of Omaney's files. See what else you can find without letting him know you've been there. Be careful. Hunter?"

"Yes, boss?" Hunter's laconic reply once again seemed at odds with the energy balled up inside him. One minute he was snarling, the next he was half asleep.

"What's wrong with you?"

Hunter narrowed his eyes, a slight flush high on his cheeks. "Nothing."

After an awkward moment of silence, Jurek decided to let the matter drop for the time being. Hunter wouldn't tell him anything until he was ready to. "Stick to the Buchanans. I want to know who they talk to, what they read, hell, what they eat for breakfast for the next few days. My gut tells me they'll break into this, being fresh on Rebecca's case. Not that our older info isn't any good," he reassured them.

Though his agency had been doing their best, they'd been running off cold kidnappings. The latest disappearance prior to Rebecca had occurred a week before they'd gotten this case. In that time, the trail had turned stale fast.

"I'm on it." J.D. shot him a mock salute, stood, then left.

Hunter waited, his amber gaze fierce. "Just how much do you know about Buchanan's family?"

"Quite a bit, actually. Years ago, Max and I worked together doing things I can't tell you about for the government. He's intelligent, built like a brick, and charming to those he wants to manipulate. And he has the ability to communicate telepathically."

Hunter didn't look surprised. "His family, are they special too?"

Ah, the crux of the matter. Jurek hadn't imagined Hunter's interest in the girl. "Max has a gift, his brother has it, and his deceased sister had it in spades. So, if I had to make a guess, on a psychic scale of one to ten, I'd say Buchanan and his brood rate an eleven."

"Psychic criminals, terrific. They're going to be a huge pain in the ass. I can feel it already, and I'm no psychic."

Again, with the denial. Jurek shook his head. "Haul that extrasensory ass out of my office and get to work." Now, how to convince the Feds to let Max play ball...

Hunter strode purposefully back to the office he rarely used and sat in his chair. Wiping absently at the dust that had settled on the arms, he noticed a folder on his desk. Yet he couldn't stop envisioning the large gray-green eyes of the woman from the warehouse. Alexandra Sainte. An eleven on the psychic scale, Jurek had said. What the hell could she do?

And why did the thought of a psychic female thrill instead of scare him?

Because it's another affirmation that you're not a freak. There are more like you out there. Rafe, J.D., Jurek, now Buchanan and his family.

Hunter had spent most of his life in hiding. But his innate gifts, his extraordinarily sharp senses and amazing speed, had made joining the Marine Corps a solid choice. Unfortunately, his consistently successful performance garnered him attention he didn't want.

From the Corps, he'd been handpicked to work in a covert sect of the CIA that protected the country from South American drug cartels and suspected terrorists. At first gratifying, the work had soon turned into more than he could bear. He'd begun losing himself in the primitive instincts of a true predator, killing without remorse, enjoying the hunt until all he could think about was killing again.

Four years ago, when Jurek Westlake had requested a sit-in on his last military debriefing, he'd been nearly out of his mind. Overstimulated to the point of constant aggression, Hunter had feared he'd never be able to live a normal life again.

Three months after meeting Jurek, the government released him. Jurek hired him before he'd realized he'd agreed to the job. And for the first time in his life, he didn't have to hide his abilities. Jurek urged him to use his talent to help, not harm.

Hunter soon found himself working alongside others with strange, unnatural abilities. Jurek applied his charm to make people do the right thing. J.D. harnessed electricity, a living conduit who had a knack for computers and the information held within them. Rafe foresaw the future. And there were others with lesser degrees of psychic ability.

But the woman. What could she do? From the first moment Hunter had seen her, he'd known there was something different about her. And the dreams he'd had compounded it. Just thinking about them made him hard.

He took her with a fierce need to possess. Not just fucking, but loving. Harder and faster, needing to spill inside her, to cement ties and own her. He came hard twice and still needed more. But that last time she surprised him. On her knees, between his legs, she'd moved closer, taking him between those thick, ripe lips, and sucked him deep.

29

"Shit." Hunter drew a deep breath and tried to ignore his horny subconscious. But no matter how much he tried to deny it, he knew she was different.

Not simply intrigued by the startling color of her eyes, he'd been drawn by something else, something he couldn't put his finger on. *And still can't. Focus on the goddamn case.*

Hunter had a job to do. He needed to organize the surveillance teams on Buchanan's people. But as he sat there and thought about those eyes that alternated from jade to emerald green, his mind drifted. Unfocused, his vision grayed and he tasted something foreign, something very much like...chocolate?

He blinked himself awake, irritated with his inability to stay on task. Worried, but not willing to admit it, he picked up the phone and ordered Williams to come up to his office for a ten o'clock meeting. Turning back to his case files, Hunter went through them line by line, looking for a clue he might have missed.

At ten-thirty, Williams entered with a harried expression on his face.

"Where the hell have you been?"

Williams stammered an apology and glanced away, as everyone did when faced with Hunter's displeasure. Only Jurek, Rafe, and J.D. maintained direct eye contact. And the Buchanans, his inner voice reminded him. They're not scared of me.

The smell of Williams' fear forced him to rein in his temper. No use alienating fellow agents, not when he needed them at their sharpest. The Buchanans weren't important. Rebecca was.

Hunter took a deep, cleansing breath. "Okay, Williams. I have a job for you and your team. We're people watching for a few days."

Chapter Two

Alex devoured the chocolate bar she'd stolen from Cole's desk. The candy melted in her mouth. Milk chocolate, her favorite. To her bemusement, the rich taste faded in comparison to her fascination with the shiny gold of her watch. That color, so vibrant, reminded her too much of the eyes of a man who wouldn't leave her thoughts.

In her mind's eye, she saw his impressive strength and his hungry gaze as he watched her. Always watching her.

"Alex? Hello?" Cole interrupted her insane fantasies, and she dropped the candy bar to the desk like a piece of hot coal. "I've been calling your name over and over again." His frown darkened when he eyed the chocolate.

"I found it," she lied, stifled a grin, and concentrated on the folder in front of her.

"Yeah, in my desk," he muttered and sat across from her. "So, what do you think about all this?"

Alex looked at a picture of Rebecca Mitchell's smiling face. "If the Mitchells haven't received a ransom note by now, they aren't going to get one. And the news Max dropped on us this morning in addition to this new file..." she paused and motioned to the folder Christine had, "...tells us Omaney may not be the only player we've got to worry about."

Cole nodded, looking disturbed. "Mrs. Mitchell comes to us

to find her missing daughter. Simple. But what's not so simple is the tie-in that Rebecca's disappearance has to six other blondes from good families, all kidnapped within the past month."

"So Westlake is in on this, what? From a federal angle?" Alex pursed her lips in thought. "I wonder how they found out about Omaney. I mean, the lipstick gave us a start. But if Luc hadn't given us his name, we'd still be in the dark."

Lucas Buchanan, Alex and Cole's cousin, had the Buchanan gift of second sight. Unlike the rest of the family, he didn't consider his special abilities as a gift, but as a curse. Only begrudgingly did he ever admit to experiencing paranormal visions. That he had called Max about something he'd seen the other day worried her.

"Luc was right about Omaney and that warehouse." Cole shook his head. "Who would have guessed? Omaney's practically the poster child for squeaky clean."

"He's in his forties and a confirmed bachelor. He's handsome, rich, influential, and a major political backer with ties to the police, government, and now a suspected slavery ring?" Alex posed the question. "I don't understand why someone with that much going for him would resort to something so incredibly *wrong*."

Cole sighed. "Just because he looks that good on the outside doesn't mean he's a Boy Scout. He hasn't gotten where he is in life by being nice." He flexed his fingers, and Alex followed the telling motion.

"Okay, just what did you see when you felt his computer keyboard?"

Cole's eyes darkened with emotion, and she wondered if he'd tell her. "Omaney and another man were engaged in some, ah, sexual play with a woman." Cole flushed.

God, she was twenty-seven. Did he really think she'd never heard the word *sex* before? What would he think if she told him she hadn't been a virgin in nearly ten years? Cole being Cole, he felt he had to protect her from everything. Alex found his attitude vastly amusing, though misplaced.

"Alex, what they did to that woman wasn't natural," he said in a troubled voice, and her amusement faded. "Though the woman didn't fight them, she didn't seem aware of her surroundings. I think they drugged her."

"Maybe that's how Rebecca's kidnappers got her away with so little fuss. They drugged her and took her out of that club." Alex glanced back down at the folder in front of her. "The last person to see Rebecca was her friend Sarah who, after giving her statement, conveniently disappeared."

"Something about Sarah Moreland doesn't smell right to me. If I had to place a bet, I'd say she knows more than she's told. That's where I'm heading, to look into Sarah's part in all this. And it's time I stepped to it." Cole stood and turned to leave, then said over his shoulder, "And stay out of my desk, you klepto."

Alex chuckled, relieved Cole could joke through the darkness settling over him. When he started to fall into one of his emotional black holes, it was hard to drag him out. If anything, he'd given himself, and her, new purpose.

She studied the missing person report in the file. Rebecca had been visiting friends in Savannah for the weekend before she went back to college. Sarah Moreland, a good friend of hers who'd moved to Charleston the year prior, had also returned for a short visit.

The last person to see them both together said that Sarah had grabbed Rebecca from the party they'd been attending to go to a ritzy nightclub downtown, a place called Seneca's.

Though Rebecca's picture had been flashed around to the employees of the popular club, no one recalled seeing her. One of the bartenders thought he might have seen Sarah, but couldn't be sure. The overwhelming amount of high-profile patrons surging through Seneca's doors had made Rebecca's face one of many that had been forgotten.

Alex frowned. Sarah Moreland might have been in on it. Maybe. Rebecca may or may not have disappeared from Seneca's, or she might have vanished anywhere between the party and the nightclub. Peter Omaney, who had been at Seneca's the night Rebecca disappeared, had a solid alibi. His handsome face could be accounted for until well past two in the morning, when he'd left the place with a nubile young redhead who swore she'd spent the night with him.

Alex poured over the information, stopping a few hours later. There was no way around it. They needed more information on Omaney. Public records and the small amount of data in this folder weren't enough.

She walked back up the stairs to her uncle's office. Christine waved her through.

Alex entered and sat across from him at his desk. "We need as much info on Omaney as we can get, and we need it fast. Cole is following the lead on Sarah Moreland."

Max nodded. "Yes, he was just letting me know. Hold on a second." He dialed and spoke comfortably with someone named Remy before he hung up.

"Who was that?"

"That," Max said with relish, "was our new IT rep. I hired Remy Davis last week when you and your brother were resting up after the Fembar investigation. Nice work, by the way."

Alex nodded, pleased that they'd salvaged Mark Fembar's reputation by successfully revealing his blackmailer—his best friend and accountant. Which made her wonder...

"Are you sure you can trust this Remy guy? I didn't even know we needed a new tech person." Buchanan Investigations had been running successfully for too long to have some new guy come in and ruin things. Though a small organization, every one of Max's employees remained loyal—a must, considering their tendency to skirt the law when necessary.

Her uncle appeared annoyed by her lack of faith. "Remy happens to be a woman, and I know she'll be a great asset to the company. Don't worry about her. Oh, and as soon as she gathers the rest of the info on Omaney that I requested *Wednesday*..." he paused, making her squirm at the reminder of the warehouse break-in, "...I'll let you know."

He opened his mouth to say something more, then closed it. The odd look on his face alarmed her, especially since he seemed focused on her.

"What? What's wrong?"

"Nothing, dear. Tell me what you thought of Westlake and his men." He leaned back in his chair, his dark eyes thoughtful.

Alex frowned at the sudden change in topic. "Ah, well, Jurek was a charming surprise. He didn't seem like the government mouthpiece I thought he'd be."

Max smiled. "Jurek is no one's lackey. I told you I worked with him a long time ago. He's a good man, but he still works with government officials I no longer trust."

"So, if you worked with Jurek, then he's like us. You said before we're not the only psychics working this case?"

Max nodded. "He's highly intuitive. He can size up your character within seconds of meeting you."

"What about that charm he fairly oozed?" she asked.

"The man's got more than a normal dose of charisma, true.

But he also has a backbone when it comes to doing what's right. Don't get me wrong, I don't necessarily trust Jurek's associates, but I trust and like him."

Alex nodded in understanding. "So does Jurek's firm operate like ours? I mean, do you think some of his people are like us?"

Max watched her with an intensity she found unnerving. "I would assume so. I'm not too familiar with his people, since I've spent the majority of my time avoiding Westlake's folks."

Unable to stop herself, Alex asked, "So you don't know anything about the men with Jurek?"

"Don't you mean, do I know anything about the giant who couldn't take his eyes off you the whole time he sat in my office?"

Alex couldn't conceal her blush. "Well, yeah. Do you know anything about him?"

Max's eyes narrowed. "Hmm, Hunter Greye, let me think."

Alex felt stupid for asking. "Never mind."

"It's good to see you so interested in our competition." Max smirked, and she wanted to smack him. "I actually did some research after they left the office. I worked with Hunter's father, retired Colonel James Greye, a long time ago. He's a good man, so I can only hope his son doesn't fall far from the tree." Max's amusement faded as he stared at her. "Still and all, watch yourself. I'm not sure I like the way Hunter fixed on you earlier. If he bothers you, let me know, and *I'll* take care of it."

Alex bristled at her uncle's concern. This was so typical, and why she hadn't asked for his permission to infiltrate that warehouse. She'd more or less blackmailed her brother into going with her, threatening to go by herself if he wouldn't help. Tired of always being pushed aside, where it was safe, Alex wanted more. She knew she could help if they'd give her the chance. Anyone could ferret information. She wanted—needed—to use the gifts God had given her.

"Alex?" Max probed, pushing at her awareness. "You'll let me know?"

Not wanting him to pull her from this case before she could prove her value, not only to him, but to her brother as well, she nodded. Besides, Hunter Greye threatened her on a level she couldn't explain. She'd keep her distance from the large man. Despite, or perhaps, because of how attractive she found him.

"Okay, Uncle Max. Whatever you say."

Three days later, Alex sat with her brother in a local coffee house down the block from the office. She glared at a nondescript gray car sitting down the street, visible through the window from her angle at the table.

"When did you first notice them?" Cole asked as he sipped his coffee.

"Just yesterday."

"Well, if they started watching you at the same time they threw someone on me, I'd say they've been tracking you since Friday." Cole appeared unconcerned.

"Why aren't you a little more bothered about this?"

"Why should I be? First of all, my tail was too obvious. I don't think Westlake meant for me to miss it. Hell, they're on the same case we are. As far as I'm concerned, the sooner either we or Westlake find Rebecca, the better." He frowned and lowered his voice. "I don't like to think of anyone at the hands of a guy like Omaney."

Alex nodded. "So a big nothing on Sarah, eh?"

"I wouldn't say that." He retrieved a baggie out of his coat pocket. Alex stared at the small change purse he held before her. "It's hers, and yes, she was nearby when Rebecca vanished from Seneca's."

"What exactly did you see?" Alex leaned closer to her brother, excited at this new break.

Cole looked around them. Seeing no one near enough to overhear, he explained, "Sarah and Rebecca left that party, just as one witness described. They arrived at Seneca's around midnight. I know because Sarah checked her watch. She was concerned about the time and nervous.

"She hurried Rebecca outside the back door of the club to go to a special party. I didn't see the man who sat waiting for Rebecca in the limo, because he sat in shadow. But Sarah knew him very well."

"Peter Omaney," Alex whispered.

"That's my take. I think she and Omaney were an item. She wanted him, and it was a familiar kind of desire, if that makes any sense."

"Right." *Not that I've felt that way myself in a long time. But I remember the thrill of wanting someone.* Alarmed at how easily her thoughts drifted to *him*, she shook off the odd remembrance of Hunter Greye and focused on this new development.

"So, how about you? What's the deal with Omaney?" Cole asked.

"Remy, the new IT rep, is quite a find. She dug up more information on this guy than I know what to do with. Apparently, Omaney has hotels and properties all over the country.

"We know he has ties to the government, but we didn't know he's been under the watchful eye of a top-secret cell in the federal bureau. Omaney keeps some unsavory companions."

Cole perked up at her words. "Really? Like who?"

"I'm not sure, yet. No names were mentioned, just vague references to someone the Feds have been trying to pin down for a very long time. They call him Wraith. Which makes me wonder..."

A mirrored confusion appeared on her brother's face. "It makes me wonder too. If Omaney's got some ties to a very bad man, why hasn't anyone moved on him before now?"

"Because, until recently, the Feds didn't know," a deep voice interrupted them.

Alex glanced up in surprise at Hunter Greye scowling down at them. He looked even sexier—*larger*—to her today than he had last week.

His eyes narrowed on her. Without asking, he pulled up a chair to join them.

Alex looked at her brother. Normally a very easy man to get along with, Cole had that look in his eyes that meant trouble for the person on the receiving end.

"What the hell do you want, Greye? This is a private conversation."

"Private?" Hunter repeated with scorn, his voice low. "If it's so private, why are you discussing Peter Omaney in a public coffee house?"

Cole leaned closer to Hunter, appearing unfazed by the man's intensity. "Peter Omaney is a public figure, Greye. We're interested in the man. Aren't we, Alex?"

Hunter's gaze swiveled to her, full of a desire he no longer banked. She could almost feel his mouth on hers, could almost taste the drugging sensuality of his kiss. Alex blinked at the sudden heat that consumed her. Then she wondered if she'd imagined the look. He continued to stare at her blandly, awaiting her response.

What the hell? Are my hormones showing me things that aren't there? "What my brother and I talk about is none of your concern, Greye." She noted the Westlake car sitting patiently outside. "But feel free to tell your drones we don't appreciate being followed."

Hunter shrugged. "You don't like the game, don't play. I'm not here to suit your whims, *Alex*," he said with a familiarity designed to annoy her.

Instead of annoying her, the use of her name on his lips made her hot.

"Why the hell are you here, Greye? What exactly do you want?" Cole asked in a low growl.

What did he want? What a joke. Hunter forced himself to look away from Cole's sister. A hard enough task on its own. The woman was drop-dead gorgeous. Long legs, pert breasts, eyes a man could drown in and lips that made him want to take and keep on taking. Since meeting her, she invaded his dreams, his waking moments... Hell, he couldn't even fantasize about a woman without an image of Alexandra Sainte being there. He'd jacked off more the past week than he had in months. He could only imagine what her watchdog of a brother would do if Hunter leaned across the table and planted one on her ripe lips.

Interesting that big brother wasn't the least intimidated by him. Hunter found himself respecting the large man even more. He'd been warily impressed by Cole's knowledge and patience around Williams' team. From the get-go, Cole had seemed to know he was being followed, but he'd let them go about their business, even slowing his pace so that Hunter's men could keep up.

Alex, on the other hand, had proven predictable. She

hadn't necessarily seemed aware of her tail but did all of her work in Buchanan's building, so her knowledge or lack thereof pertaining to the case had been inconclusive.

As Hunter wondered how to reply to Cole's gauntlet, he couldn't help glancing at Alex again. He'd been distracted since he'd met her, with those odd attacks on his senses. Just moments after she and her brother had sat in here, he'd gotten the strongest taste of coffee in his mouth.

Hunter didn't drink coffee.

He forced himself to look away from her mesmerizing gaze and turned to her brother, only to see the same damned gray-green eyes. "I think you need to understand something. Westlake Enterprises is working in conjunction with the government. There are lives at stake. So if you find something that might help us catch the bastards taking these women, you need to give it to us."

Cole glared. "Why do you think I let your agents follow me? I want Rebecca and the others found. I'm not interested in a pissing contest to see who's in charge of what."

"Good. Because I *am* in charge. I don't want to have to watch out for you Buchanans running underfoot while I conduct this investigation. We're running out of time. If you find anything we need to know, you'd better share it. Next time I won't ask nicely." He stood to leave, ignoring Cole's profane response.

He stopped and, against his better judgment, faced the gorgeous Amazon now glaring at him. He sighed. "Hazelnut, right?" He looked down at her cup.

She blinked in surprise and answered warily, "Yeah."

He left the shop without another word, aware of her with every step. *Good one, Hunter. Now she knows you're on to her mind games.* He swore to himself as he started his truck and

41

drove back to the office.

He'd spent a considerable amount of time dwelling on the odd sensations he'd been having since his last encounter with Alexandra Sainte. Lust aside, they shared a connection he planned on severing pronto. He needed all of his attention focused on this case. The fact that, in one month, seven women had disappeared, and no one had been able to find a trace of them, both angered and challenged him. His hunting instincts on alert, he could almost smell the scent of his prey in the air, just around the next bend as he followed the elusive kidnapper's clues.

Between J.D.'s efforts and his own progress, they knew enough to set them on a course of action. But the knowledge didn't comfort the way it should have.

Every one of the girls kidnapped came from a rich family and were alike—blonde hair, shapely builds, intelligent and well-spoken. Peter Omaney definitely had involvement with at least some of the women gone missing, including Rebecca Mitchell. However, Omaney only made up half the team that Hunter now pursued.

According to their sources, Wraith was likely involved.

Known to traffic drugs and illegal arms, Wraith had allegedly moved on to bigger and better things, namely attractive women to buy and sell for the right price. Who better to serve as Wraith's contact than Peter Omaney, a respectable businessman apparently above the law, who had contacts in high places?

Hunter parked his truck and walked back to his office. Nailing Omaney would be a feat in itself. The man had absolutely nothing dirty that they could find. If not for J.D.'s wizardry with the computer, they wouldn't have gotten as far as they had tying him to the disappearances.

Omaney's connection to several of the missing women's families wouldn't be worth squat in a court of law. That he'd been present at the same places from where the women had gone missing could be chalked up as coincidence. The rich and famous certainly frequented many of the same circles.

Still, Omaney was only a stepping-stone toward the real villain—Wraith. In order to find those women and stop this rash of kidnappings, they'd have to take down a legend.

But then, perhaps they could use a legend to take down one. That thought in mind, he headed to Jurek with an idea.

Chapter Three

Alex stared after Hunter, trying to understand the heat that still sparked from his presence. Conscious of her brother's frown, she tried to soothe his anger. "Just ignore him, Cole. He's just a big gust of wind." *Yeah, like a tornado.* "What's the worst he can do? He can't force us to go through him on every step of this case. Besides, I might just have an idea on how we can get the ball rolling a little faster."

"Let's go."

She followed Cole out of the shop and drove them back to the office. As they rode the elevator, she outlined a rough plan, one that had real merit.

"No." Cole shook his head as they exited on Max's floor. "Absolutely not."

"But, Cole, it's a good plan. It'll get us face time with Omaney, and it might just lead us to Rebecca." She tried to catch up to his hurried stride.

He ignored her.

Angered at the stubbornness of men in general, she used her mind to trip him and received a glare for her efforts.

"Oh, fine then," she huffed and moved around him. "I'll just ask Uncle Max what he thinks."

But as she drew closer to Max's doorway, she slowed when

she saw him comforting Mrs. Mitchell in his office.

Max urged the woman to dry her tears while he patted her back. He looked up with relief at Alex's approach. Christine was nowhere to be found. *"Thank God. Give me a hand here,"* he sent Alex.

Hard on her heels, Cole entered the office as well, and the two sat quietly while Gina Mitchell composed herself.

"Gina, I'd like you to hear what we've got so far on the case." He added to Alex, *"Try to give her a little hope."*

Alex cleared her throat and spoke softly. "Mrs. Mitchell? I'll give you the condensed version of what we know. Sometime last Monday night, your daughter visited Seneca's nightclub with her friend Sarah Moreland. We think Sarah was involved in Rebecca's disappearance." She asked her uncle, *"Should I tell her about Omaney?"*

"Yes."

"Peter Omaney has a part to play in her abduction as well, but we're not sure exactly what yet."

Gina Mitchell nodded, her face drawn. "Good, good. Know that if you need anything—money, support, anything—all you have to do is ask. I want my baby back," she said quietly, though with a steely undertone that contradicted her frail appearance.

"Gina, have the Feds come up with anything yet?" Max asked gently.

She shook her head. "Not that I know of. I know Harlan's been working hand in hand with them and Westlake's group for a while now. But I truly believe that the more people we have working on this, the better."

Max nodded. "You're right of course. I know I don't have to tell you to keep this quiet. Omaney's going to be a hard nut to crack, but we'll do it. We can't afford to let him know we're on to him."

"Don't worry about me." Gina stood, and Max stood with her. "Please keep doing what you're doing. I want to find Rebecca safe and sound." Her eyes filled again, and Max escorted her to the elevator.

"That poor woman." Cole shook his head.

"It's so sad," Alex agreed. "But she's right. The more people working this case, the better. It's too bad we can't convince Westlake to work with us."

"Yeah, well, I'm not too proud to share information if it will help us find Rebecca. Greye can go screw himself," Cole muttered.

Max returned and sat behind his desk. "Thanks for that, Alex. Gina's having a tough time right now."

"About that, Uncle Max. I've got an idea that may get us closer to finding her daughter."

Max glanced from Alex to Cole, apparently seeing the disapproval on her brother's face. He sighed. "This ought to be good."

"We know Omaney is involved in this up to his eyeballs. Let's throw him a ringer. Me." She managed a sly grin, praying that just once, her uncle would view her as more than his dead sister's baby girl. "Think about it. I had Remy give me what Jurek's folks know. And you know what? I look exactly like the other women taken. We know Omaney took Rebecca from Seneca's. According to his assistant, he'll be in town this weekend. Why not put me in the crowd? I'll get into his loop and give us an inside look at the man."

Max remained silent.

"She wants to play decoy and get Omaney sniffing around

her," Cole growled. "I don't like it. Sure, I can see Omaney interested. They all are." He snorted. "But this is crazy. What are the odds he'll grab her after taking Rebecca from the exact same spot just a week ago?"

Max assessed her. "Quite good, actually. Your sister is right. She and Rebecca look enough alike to be sisters. Just like the others taken. With the right background, she might work as bait."

"It's too dangerous," Cole insisted.

She would have argued her point when her uncle interrupted. To her shock, Max took her side. "In two weeks time, Wraith is holding an auction. He's going to sell the women he's kidnapped to the highest bidder."

"How do you know?"

"That information came from Luc. I've already informed Jurek."

"Shit." Cole rubbed his temples.

Max said quietly, "You have to let go sometime. I know this stretches way beyond Alex's normal involvement in the business. But we'll need to move fast if we want to find Rebecca alive." He took a deep breath, then added in a flinty voice, "Cole, by the end of this week, I'll expect you to have a job in Seneca's, where Alex will work her way to Omaney's side."

Cole glared at his uncle, his jaw tight. Alex sensed an unspoken argument, and then her brother stormed from the room.

Alex faced her uncle, thrilled to be a part of things, for once. "I think it's the right thing to do. I promise I won't screw it up."

Max nodded, his familiar arrogance oddly comforting. "You're damned right you won't screw it up. You're my niece.

You'll do fine. But, honey, Cole's right about this being dangerous. This is more than a typical information grab-and-go. Study the files Remy gave us. You need to know Omaney inside and out. You'll be the key to getting us closer to Rebecca." He cleared his throat. "Luc mentioned you might help us out on this one."

That quickly, her excitement faded. "So the only reason you're letting me do this is that according to Luc, I've already done it?"

"Yes." Max made no apology.

"Glad to know you have such faith in me."

"Oh, honey, this isn't about faith. I worry about you. Miranda left you and your brother in my keeping. You're my—"

"If you say baby girl, I'm going to seriously lose it. Dammit, why don't you worry this much about Cole?"

"Who says I don't?" he responded with a quirk to his lips. "Get over your mad, Alex. Read about Omaney. Remy's put together a surprisingly thorough dossier."

"I will." *And I'll show you both I don't need your smothering protection any longer. My gifts are just as strong as yours.*

"Good." When she didn't move, his eyes narrowed. "Is there anything else on your mind?" He grew very still. "Has Greye been bothering you?"

Before this meeting, it had been on the tip of her tongue to confide in her uncle about her recent altercation with Hunter to get his perspective. But knowing he trusted more in Luc's vision than in her ability to take care of herself, she kept quiet. Alex had no intention of jeopardizing her chance to work this case. Nor did she want to admit she couldn't handle Greye. This was her opportunity to show her family she'd finally grown up. That her abilities were just as strong as Cole's and her cousin's.

"I'm just thinking about the case, Uncle Max."

"Fine," he said, but she had the feeling he didn't believe her. To her relief, he scowled at his computer monitor. "Now get out and get busy. I have things of my own to do."

She quickly left his office and returned to her own. Wanting to study the fat folder on her desk, she couldn't help dwelling on her brother. According to Christine, he'd left the building, clearly upset.

She couldn't blame Cole for being protective. Since the death of their parents sixteen years ago, Cole had been her rock. Max had taken them in and cared for them like a father, but Cole and she shared a special bond.

Cole felt responsible for her, though she'd been working very hard to make him see her as an adult. For a while, she'd thought about leaving the firm and working on her own. But having to hide her abilities all the time would stifle her. Alex kept thinking that the next case would be her big break. She'd been hoping for six years.

What would it take to make Cole back off? She had her own apartment, her own job as an investigator, and had reached the age of twenty-seven without suffering too much harm. Hadn't she taken down those men in the warehouse last week?

She forced herself to admit that the security guards had been fairly weak. Against a stronger foe, a man like Hunter, she probably wouldn't stand a chance. *Physically, that is. Mentally, I could kick his ass.*

Psychic ability ran strong in her family, on both her mother's and father's sides. Alex concentrated on a pen that had rolled to the floor. It suddenly lifted into the air and flew to her desk. A pen weighed little, a man much more. But in fight mode, Alex had learned to utilize all her defenses. While Hunter Greye might outmuscle her, she had a few tricks up her sleeve, and Alex played to win. The next time they met, she intended to have the last word. One way or the other.

Two days later, Hunter stood grimfaced in front of a slate blue door and pounded again. He smelled lavender and clenched his jaw at the effort it took to focus on his present course of action. He knew the damned woman was home.

When no one answered after a few more minutes, he set to work. The lock proved no problem, her security alarm even less of one. He'd have a talk with her about that...*afterward.*

Hunter had tried, but he could no longer avoid the inevitable. This had to stop. He moved silently and swiftly through her open rooms, noting the tidiness of her apartment. Alexandra Sainte decorated sparsely but with a warmth that was inviting.

An eclectic mix of styles accented the cozy feel of a living room well used. A plush leather sofa and matching chair congregated around a teak coffee table covered with home design magazines and the occasional fitness rag. A few plants, all healthy and thriving, sat in her picture window, overlooking a common courtyard. The few bookcases along a far wall boasted an assortment of titles, none of which indicated her preference of reading material.

He entered her spotless kitchen. The counters appeared clean, as did her pristine white cabinets. The ceramic sink remained free of dirty dishes. Not even a speck of dirt in the drain. *Dear God, did anyone actually live here?* Then the scent of lavender hit him hard. Again. His pulse raced, his body tightened, and pure, sensual need spiked his blood.

Swearing under his breath, he continued his search for the feminine bane of his existence. He turned into a hallway off the living room and stilled. He could smell her there, could almost feel her delicate energy in the air.

Time to tie up a few loose ends.

Williams's crew had given up their efforts at discreet surveillance and tailed Alex outright. Tonight, Hunter decided to take care of watching over Ms. Sainte personally. Professionally. *Finally.*

The sound of water splashing drew him down the hallway and through an untidy bedroom—a surprise inconsistent with the rest of the house. He walked through the doorway into her bathroom and froze.

Even though he'd been expecting it, the vision of Alex covered in bubbles struck him with the force of a physical blow. Surrounded by lavender and warmed by the humidity in the intimate bathroom, Hunter was overwhelmed with a sudden need to touch her golden skin, wet and shining before him. Calling on every ounce of discipline he possessed, Hunter forced himself to remain still and studied the sleepy beauty he couldn't get out of his mind.

A man would have to be blind not to appreciate her looks— golden hair streaked with honey, exotically slanted eyes that hinted at mystery, and full lips promising everything a man might want. Her body curved in all the right places, yet had a toned toughness that told Hunter she wouldn't break, even under a bit of rough handling.

The thought aroused him into taking a step forward. Desire engulfed him, and he literally ached, needing to touch her, to be inside that glorious body and discover just what it was about her that captivated him. Only one woman had ever come this close to making him lose control, and look at how that had turned out.

Angered at reminders of the poor choices he'd once made,

he locked down his traitorous body and forced himself to handle this—*her.*

"All right, Sainte. Enough is enough," he growled.

She shrieked in surprise and sloshed in the tub, allowing him glimpses of slick flesh while she tried to gain her feet. Forcing himself to ignore the impulse to reach out and touch, he handed her a towel.

She grabbed it from him and hastily wrapped it around herself. "What— Who—" She took a deep breath. "How the hell did you get in my apartment?"

He frowned. "You need to update your security. Pretty sad that I managed your locks in less than a minute."

Slicking her hair back, she regarded him with caution and kept a firm hand on the top of her towel.

He forced himself to look no lower than her chin. "We need to talk."

"No shit." Instead of the fear he assumed he'd face, the woman had the nerve to step out of the tub right in front of him. No more than three inches remained between him and her delectable body draped with a thin towel. "You can't just barge into private property whenever you feel like it, Greye. Now get the hell out of my bathroom. Get the hell out of my apartment!"

"I don't think you understand me, angel. *I'm* here to talk. All you need to do is listen." He stepped closer and inhaled her scent—feminine, floral and damned arousing. Pressed so close, she had to notice his reaction. When her eyes widened, he gave her a grim smile, caught by her tremulous gaze. "I didn't want to do it this way," he said darkly. "But you keep playing your games."

"Games?" she parroted, her gaze glued to his mouth.

Disturbingly pleased he wasn't the only one affected,

Hunter strove to focus on the topic at hand. "The coffee? The chocolate? The feel of your soft skin under my hands? Projecting your bullshit is only distracting me from the mission at hand."

She blinked up at him. "What are you talking about?"

"You know." He couldn't help himself and latched onto the firm strength of her shoulders. His thumb brushed the side of her breast, and she gasped. "You're a beautiful woman, and you know it. You don't need to play games to get my attention. Just let me handle this job, and I'll give you exactly what you've been asking for."

Her apparent anger stirred him past reason. Alexandra Sainte in nothing but a towel was bad enough, but in a passionate temper, her energy seethed and drew him like a moth to flame.

"Why you arrogant—"

The little witch thought to challenge him even now? *The hell she did.*

He kissed past her denial, knowing she didn't mean it. He could all but sense her arousal as it pulsed through him. Feminine need and anger warred until her rage surrendered to the attraction between them. Everything she felt, Hunter felt as well, until he regained control once more, taking charge of his emotions.

Licking his way past her lips, he plunged his tongue inside and groaned. She tasted like candy, sweet and fresh. Angling closer, he ravaged her mouth, not satisfied until she panted, her taut breasts heaving against his chest.

Yanking the towel from her, he immediately cupped her firm globes, taken with the full swells and hard peaks beading for him. Reason lost to madness as he gave in to the instinctive need to take more.

Breaking from her lips, he leaned down and took her nipple in his mouth. He wanted to purr with satisfaction when she gasped his name and tugged his hair. Instead of pulling him away, she pressed him closer, shifting hungrily beneath him.

"God, Hunter. What are you doing to me?" She moaned again, soft and pliant under his hands.

"You feel like silk," he murmured, tending to her other breast. He ran a hand over her hip and belly, seeking the heat between her legs. Thrilled when he found what he sought, he thrust one finger deep.

Alex let go of his head to grip his shoulders. "Hunter, please."

He didn't know if she pleaded for more or for him to stop, but he didn't care. He would stop after he'd made his point...just as soon as he could remember what that was.

"You're hot and wet, angel. So pretty under my hands," he whispered, chancing a glance into her eyes. They darkened, gleaming like emerald green pools, slumberous yet lit with sexual energy. "Yes, that's it. Follow my lead. Let me take you."

"No, I..." She broke off when he shifted his thumb and began stroking that tight bundle of nerves at her core. "Oh, Hunter. Oh, yes. Please," she begged.

Yes. Please her. Rip away the clothing separating you and please yourself as well.

He pushed at Alex's will until she crumbled under his touch, helpless to stop the desire exploding throughout her body. She cried his name as she came, stirring his temper anew. God, he hurt. The need to possess her was animalistic, an intuitive need to conquer, the way he used to feel during his days in the military...and during his courtship of Anna.

Not liking this lack of control where she was concerned, Hunter strove to find distance. He withdrew his hand from between her legs and took a step back. Reaching down for her towel, he found it and wrapped it around her.

He made his second big mistake of the night when he looked into her eyes, because he saw not just an erotic playmate, but a vulnerable woman staring out at him. Not liking this need to offer comfort, he strengthened his inner defense with a harsh offense.

"Think that can tide you over until we've found Rebecca?" he asked. "Or do I need to fuck you to get the job done?"

The hurt on her face made him feel as if he'd kicked a kitten. But he should have remembered kittens have claws.

Lightning fast, Alex slapped him hard across the face. She fisted her hand by her side, and he wondered if she meant to hit him again, and if he should let her. "I didn't ask you here. I didn't ask for *this*."

"Sure you did. Tell me you didn't want it."

She paled.

"That's what I thought. Now listen up, angel, and listen good. I don't have time for your petty mind games. Quit screwing with me. And don't pretend you don't know what I mean."

"I don't." Yet she sounded less certain than she'd been before.

"Yes, you do." *Dammit.* Did she think he was playing? "There's a time and a place for fun. But not during a mission. I had the impression your uncle feels the same way. You put this case in jeopardy, and you'll answer to more than me." Unable to stop himself, he pinned her fists to her sides and kissed her again, a hard reminder that, as much as he might wish it, he wasn't immune to her charms. "You're good, but a piece of ass isn't worth some innocent woman's life. Rebecca is all that matters right now. You get me, angel?"

Alex tried to break free, but couldn't under his firm grip. She scowled like a thundercloud. "Oh, I get you."

Hunter's pulse raced. He couldn't have explained why, but Alex in a fury turned him on like nothing else. Which made no sense and had no place in his life, especially not now.

The plan he and Jurek had concocted would work, but only if the players kept strict attention on the game. Hunter wouldn't allow anyone, not even Max Buchanan's sexy niece, to endanger the mission.

With regret that he couldn't ease his present sexual frustration, he let her go and stepped back. When she made no move to follow, he nodded. "Glad to see we're on the same page."

She didn't say anything and continued to stare holes through him. Even annoyed, she captivated him, and she wasn't even trying.

He sighed. "Let the big boys do what we do best. You find anything we might need, let us know." He paused, realizing he might have been overly harsh. It wasn't all her fault he couldn't control his dick. "Don't worry, angel. When I'm done, we'll pick up where we left off. Count on it."

Hunter turned and left without a backwards glance, knowing that if he looked at her again, he might not have the willpower to leave. And God knew, someone needed to think with more than their hormones on this case. The Bureau hadn't been able to pin a thing on Wraith in more than a decade. Omaney was squeaky clean. And in two more weeks, seven innocent women would be sold off like cattle. For Hunter and the others to succeed, they needed to be at the top of their game. Not pawns on someone else's board, no matter how much his body might want otherwise.

Chapter Four

Cole kept his grin in place even as he seethed inwardly. This had to be the most asinine thing his sister had ever done. He still couldn't believe his uncle had sanctioned it. And Luc, that little prick, had managed to avoid him for days. What a perfect time to embrace the *curse* he'd always hated and thrust Alex into the lion's den.

Cole occupied himself behind the bar and kept an eye out. In the three days he'd been bartending, Omaney had failed to show, but rumor had it he'd visit tonight. Alex had already made appearances last night and the night before and drew men to her with ease. It didn't help that Cole saw her holding her own. He felt his parents turning over in their graves at their little girl working men like a pro.

Jane, his manager, patted his ass *again* as she sashayed past him. A patron at the end of the bar noticed and gave him a shit-eating grin. Cole glared back, but the damage had been done. Damn, he hadn't wanted his cousin Thorne to see that.

At least Alex had him and Thorne for backup. His cousin's job to shadow Alex gave Cole some much-needed relief. Cole watched him leave the bar to mingle, making another pass through the place. Thorne Buchanan could be a real pain in the ass, but he fit in with the crowd in this club as if born to a silver spoon. His intensity, not to mention his dark masculinity and tall frame—according to Alex—attracted others with ease.

So long as he keeps the monsters from my sister. And therein lies the problem, because the stubborn idiot wants their attention in order to nab the worst of the lot. Reluctantly pushing his reservations aside, Cole set to work. The next hour breezed by. Until his sister arrived, it was business as usual. He reluctantly admitted his sordid fascination with the club, unable to tear his gaze from the glitz all around.

The rich, the infamous, and the famous caroused together. It was no wonder celebrities and bigwigs alike frequented Seneca's. The owner, a mogul in the music industry, had purchased the club for his third wife, a twenty-one-year-old porn star. The scandal of their marriage had made tabloid heaven, but didn't deter patrons from attending the hot nightspot. Hell, with this crowd, the gossip had probably attracted them.

Just like it would soon draw Alexandra Tyrell, a model from a prominent family, courtesy of Gina Mitchell's contacts. Alex had the proper paperwork and electronic trail to make her cover convincing, as well as a few runway shots quickly taken a few days past, putting her somewhere in France before she'd arrived in Savannah.

From the attention she received, Cole wondered if his sister would in fact have been better off as a model. Though Alex worked for Buchanan Investigations, she'd never before been so active in her role as an agent. Of the two of them, Cole took the risks, while Alex remained safe—where she belonged—behind a desk, *far away from here.*

"Yo, Bloody Mary for me and these two," a drunken playboy ordered.

After serving yet another loser, Cole checked his watch. Midnight, already. As if on cue, Peter Omaney entered the club through a private entrance. He cut through the crowd without trouble, and people greeted him like royalty.

A glance at the stairwell showed Thorne talking on his cell phone. Minutes later, a gorgeous woman in a tight red dress pushed past him toward the bar. Several people around her stopped and stared. Omaney looked as if he'd been pole-axed. *Great, now Omaney will be too distracted to focus on Alex...*

"Shit!" That was his sister parading around like an upscale call girl. He quickly informed a coworker that he planned on a short break and moved to the edge of the bar where he could see her better.

He couldn't stop goggling at Alex, wishing he had a jacket to cover her from head to toe. Tonight, she didn't look like anyone's little sister. She must have poured that dress on. He didn't know how she could breathe in it, let alone walk in the thing. The dress barely reached mid-thigh. It shimmered under the flashing lights of the club. She'd done something wild with her hair. The color looked white-blonde, and she'd pulled it up to expose her slim neck while strands dangled from a comb, licking at the back of her neck and shoulders.

The dress's plunging neckline was bad enough. Then she turned around to speak with someone. The damned thing had almost no back, resting just above her backside. *And those heels.* How the hell could she defend herself wearing three-inch spiked heels? Mission or no mission, he needed to save his sister from the dozens of male predators just waiting to take advantage. This was too much.

"Whoa, buddy." Thorne suddenly stood in front of him and spoke in a low voice. "I admit, it took me a minute to realize that's Alex. She wore tamer stuff yesterday, for sure. But she's working. Hey, it's all for a good cause, right? Don't worry. I'm not taking my eyes off her. Like all the other dogs in this place," he muttered.

Cole scowled at his cousin, forcing himself to look away from his sister before we went blind. Who knew she had a body like that? God, he wanted to erase tonight and start over.

Thorne groaned. "I'm never letting Storm do anything like this."

Cole snorted. "As if you could stop her. Your sister's been of her own mind since she was ten." Thorne's younger sister had a wild streak very similar to Alex's. *Bad Buchanan blood. Thanks a lot, Mom.*

"Yeah, well, I'd better go mingle so I can keep up with *your* sister. A red dress? Like waving a flag at a roomful of bulls. Damn." Thorne strode back into the crowd, following Alex into the swell.

Cole took a moment to compose himself and resumed his position behind the bar. He continued to serve drinks, knowing Alex would make contact with him. He'd play it cool, but he planned to tell her what he thought of this stupidity later.

It didn't take her more than an hour before she stood in front of him, waving a ten dollar bill. "I'd like a white wine," she said in a sultry voice that sounded very unlike her.

Cole forced himself to nod. Up close, he could see the subtle changes she'd made to her appearance. She'd applied some dark color to her eyes that made them look more exotic and mysterious. Her cheekbones looked higher, her brows more defined. Alex's lips were slick and red, and he had to refrain from bashing the head of the man next to her, who wouldn't stop staring.

"Wine's on the house. Enjoy yourself, sugar," Cole said with a grin that didn't meet his eyes. Alex's smile faltered before she brightened the wattage and turned away with a glass and a thank you.

It took another half hour before Omaney wrangled an introduction.

Soon enough, the pair headed up the side stairs, past a pair of guards, to a private floor. From this angle, Cole wouldn't be able to see her very well. Thorne met his gaze and winked before following his cousin up the stairs without a problem.

Grabbing Jane's arm the next time she passed him, Cole excused himself with the promise to grab more towels from the storage room. Once there, he took a small earpiece from his pocket and settled in to listen.

Alex smiled up at Peter Omaney. It was a shame he looked even better in person than he did in his photographs. Tall and dark, with engaging blue eyes and a dimple that flashed when he smiled, he was the epitome of charm.

She felt Peter's hand on her back as he escorted her up the stairs. He had a large hand, soft and warm. But his touch didn't have half the heat Hunter's did. And once again her mind wandered to that overbearing, obnoxious man.

Since their last explosive encounter, she'd put all her energies into pouring over every detail of Peter Omaney's life. She knew of his likes and dislikes, about his distant relatives and his job. The past few nights at Seneca's had given her insights into his shadowy peers, the many women he'd been with, and the men who considered themselves his friends.

If she were lucky, tonight might also be the start to revealing more of Omaney's associates, those who lived in the darker corners of the world, where Rebecca might be found.

"Here you go, Alex." Peter sat her at his table, just one of five on this level. Big money and influence lorded above the peons on the floor. She didn't see her brother by the bar and prayed he wouldn't do anything reckless. *Like storm up here and save me from this creep. As much as I don't want to admit it, I'd welcome the rescue. Peter Omaney is bad news. I can feel it.*

He sat next to her, then reached over to take her hand. He kissed the back of it and held on. His gaze traced her features, but didn't roam lower than her chin. The consummate gentleman. "You are absolutely gorgeous," he said without blinking. "How is it I've never seen you here before?"

Alex subtly tugged at her hand, relieved when he let her go. She stuck to her script and answered, "I've recently returned to the states. I spent the past few months in Europe. My modeling career is really taking off," she said excitedly. "But I can't say I've never seen *you* before. You're even better looking than your photos, which is saying a lot."

Peter took a swallow of scotch. "Flatterer," he said with a smile.

She heard a hint of the South in his deep voice and again wondered why a man like this, a man with such charm, polish, and standing, would do something so awful as kidnapping.

"I try." She drank from her wine slowly, licking her lips as she finished. His gaze locked onto her mouth. Alex needed to make an impression on this man without being too easy. Conscious of the listening device fixed to the front of her dress, camouflaged as a rhinestone, she kept her arms free from hindering his view of her décolletage.

"Tell me, Peter. How can a man as attractive and smart as you possibly be here all alone?" Alex leaned closer.

He subtly glanced down her dress. She reminded herself to play it cool. *He's buying it. Don't screw it up, Alex. You can do this.*

"But, sugar, if I'd come with someone else, I wouldn't have been free to find you," he said smoothly.

She managed to continue their inconsequential small talk

for another hour. She mostly listened while he spoke.

"I've been talking all night, Alex. Why don't you tell me more about you? Where are you staying while you're here?"

Alex sipped slowly at her second glass of wine. She'd been very careful with her drinks, never completely taking her hand or gaze from her glass. Thorne had somehow made his way upstairs and sat across the floor with two beautiful redheads while he kept a surreptitious eye on her.

"I'm staying at the Formati. I hear it's the best place in town." Alex smiled and waited for his answer, knowing what it should be.

"The Formati, oh yes. Benjamin Anthony, the owner, is a very good friend of mine." He watched her absorb the news with a calculating gleam in his eyes.

"Really?"

The Formati Hotel had appeared in the files she and Cole had stolen from his warehouse. Rebecca had also been staying at the Formati before she'd disappeared.

"Ben and I go way back," Peter continued. "He's a helluva guy. Perhaps, if you have some time tomorrow, we could meet for lunch and I could introduce you?"

Alex knew of Peter's tie to the hotel owner. The pair had roomed together at Harvard before finding one another again five years ago when they had partnered up to buy the Formati Suites. Peter obviously preferred that his partnership be kept silent.

"That would be nice." Alex looked down at his watch and gasped. "I can't believe it's already after two. I've got to get back to my hotel and get some sleep. I'm supposed to meet with my agent tomorrow to discuss my cover shoot for *Chic.*"

Peter nodded and stood with her. "Let's go."

She paused. This wasn't in the script. She was supposed to say goodbye, part ways, and leave. He wasn't supposed to come with her. "Please, I don't want to take you away from your fun."

"It's not fun without you. Come on, honey. I'll see you safely to the hotel." He took her by the elbow and walked with her down the stairs. She could feel Thorne's stare burning a hole in her back and knew her brother would be beyond riled should she deviate from the plan.

Still, what harm could Omaney really do, considering the listening device on her dress? If he got too pushy, she had Cole, Thorne, and Max for help. A glance behind her showed Thorne following several strides away. The disapproval on his face stung as well as irritated. Yet *another* male telling her what to do.

"Thanks so much, Peter. I wasn't looking forward to a cab."

They pressed through the crowd toward a private exit blocked by a hulking doorman.

"Mr. Omaney." He nodded to Peter and smiled at Alex while he held the door for them. Outside, a limo waited several yards away. In minutes, the limo rounded to pick them up. Alex knew it was do or die time. She took a deep breath and entered ahead of Peter. Seated, she glanced around her, hoping to find something to take back to her brother. She could only imagine what he'd *see* off something from Peter's private vehicle. Unfortunately, she saw nothing to take.

Peter sat next to her, and the limo rolled away. "Tired?" he asked. He stretched out an arm along the back of her seat and toyed with a lock of her hair. Before she could say anything, he lowered his hand to her neck and began rubbing.

Had she not known better, Alex might have thought she'd met Mr. Perfect. Charming and handsome, polite and gentlemanly, Peter Omaney hadn't put one foot out of place tonight. She wondered if those had been Rebecca's thoughts before she'd been taken against her will.

"You're so tense." Peter frowned.

Of course she was tense. She sat next to a man who looked like an angel, but was suspected of human trafficking. *Don't screw this up, idiot. You wanted out from behind the desk, now you've got it. Act.* She eased her shoulders down and relaxed into her role.

Alex winked at him and his frown receded. A glance out the window behind him showed her that they'd almost reached the hotel. *Thank God.*

"I'm just worried that if I'm too relaxed, I'll fall asleep and miss my alarm tomorrow," she teased as his fingers skimmed her jaw. She shuddered, and Peter chuckled, misconstruing her disgust for arousal.

He leaned close to nip her earlobe, then whispered, "I can make sure that doesn't happen if I wake up next to you."

Crap. Her brother, Thorne, and Max were listening to this. How best to play the part?

He took hold of her hand and placed it in his lap.

"Oh!" She squeezed without thinking.

He groaned. "Is that a yes?" he asked and sucked on her earlobe.

Alex jerked her hand away. "I wish." She sighed. "Not tonight, Peter. I really do need to focus on tomorrow. This shoot can make or break my career. But does that invitation to lunch still stand?"

She must have sounded sincere, because Peter nodded with satisfaction. He rapped on his window and the door opened. His chauffer assisted her out of the vehicle.

"Until tomorrow, Alex. I'll leave you a message at the desk.

Forgive me if I don't see you to the door," Peter said ruefully.

Alex waved and strode with confidence into the hotel, quaking on the inside. She couldn't believe she'd pulled it off. Her first successful undercover mission. Now if she could just make it to her room without throwing up.

Hunter seethed. What the hell was Buchanan Investigations up to? They stood on the fourteenth floor of the posh hotel while he waited for J.D. to work his mojo. Aware of all the electronics in the place, and specifically of the cameras in place on each floor, J.D. concentrated and disabled the devices long enough for them to enter Alex's suite undetected.

Once inside the hotel room, J.D. nodded at Hunter. "We're clean." He referred to the surveillance devices. "Now, remember, keep your temper," J.D. cautioned, as he'd been cautioning since he'd called Hunter an hour ago.

Hunter couldn't believe Alex thought she could get away with it. What the hell did she think she was doing, cozying up to Peter Omaney? Didn't she realize Omaney ate blondes for breakfast? Did she really think some harmless flirting would satisfy a man like him, let alone have him spilling his guts about his every misdeed?

Thinking about the last time he'd been in a confined area with the little witch, Hunter closed his eyes and prayed for patience to keep things easy between them. *No more touching, and definitely no more kissing.*

He opened his eyes and growled, "You'd better go get her. There's no telling what I'll do if I go in there."

"I'm telling you, buddy. If you could have seen her in that little red number she was wearing. *Hot damn.*" J.D. fanned himself and moved to retrieve Alex. "You most definitely would not be thinking about strangling her."

Not strangling her, shoving some sense—and several other body parts—into her. Hunter forced himself to remain calm, to call on his training and discipline. He wouldn't allow any interference in this investigation. Lives were on the line. He refused to contemplate the fact that thoughts of Alex and Omaney together made him see red, then green.

J.D. knocked on her bedroom door.

"Cole?" Alex sounded groggy.

Hunter heard the door open, then Alex hissing something before slamming it shut. J.D. reappeared and plunked down in the taupe sofa facing away from Alex's bedroom.

"She'll be out momentarily. For the record, that dress she wore tonight had nothing on what I just saw." J.D. sighed with pleasure.

Fury rose like a tidal wave inside him. "You'd better start thinking with your brain instead of your dick, or you're off this case. We've got a job to do."

J.D. glared. "Get a grip, Hunter. Some of us can appreciate beauty without losing our heads. Or our control," he added, his eyes bright with challenge.

Hunter would have responded, but Alex joined them. She wore a large, fluffy white robe and a glare hot enough to melt ice cream.

"You again. What a surprise," she said in a flat tone.

"Tell me about it." Hunter wished he had something more clever to say, but he had a hard time looking past her smart mouth just begging for a kiss. God, the fantasies he'd had of those lips hugging his cock...

Silence filled the room until J.D. coughed. "Alex, fancy meeting you here."

She scowled and sat with a huff in the chair adjacent to the couch. Her robe parted at the knee. Hunter was quick to follow the flash of bare skin. Alex flushed when she noted his fixed gaze and hurriedly tucked the material around her.

"Do you mind?" she asked testily. With her hair tumbling over her shoulders and her face flushed, she looked as if she'd just left a lover behind.

The thought made him want to punch something, but, conscious of J.D.'s interest, he pulled hard on his control. "Mind? Not at all," Hunter said smoothly. "Now, why don't you tell us what the hell you're doing nosing around Omaney? Didn't I tell you before not to interfere with our investigation?"

"I am doing my damnedest to find Rebecca Mitchell, you jerk. Believe it or not, Buchanan Investigations wants to find her alive and well. Take your pissing contest elsewhere, Greye. You can't corner the market on justice."

Hunter approached until he loomed over her. He couldn't decide whether to throttle her or make love to her. A glance at J.D. showed the man captivated by their byplay. The jackass wiggled his eyebrows, as if to say, follow your own damned advice. *Hell.* He'd have to settle for verbal castigation. "We? So I take it your brother's around here somewhere? Your other guard sure as shit left in a hurry. Nice to know you're well protected." He couldn't help his sarcasm, angry all over again at thoughts of Alex in harm's way.

She didn't respond.

"Alex?" Familiar with the mutinous set of her mouth, he knew he would need to prod her into an answer. He crouched down in front of her at eye-level and used the excuse to touch her, stroking soft blonde hair that felt like satin. She jumped under his palm, and he pulled back. "Answer me, or do you want me to ask again, *my* way?" He centered his gaze on her mouth, his intent clear.

She quickly stood and moved behind the chair, putting distance between them. "Cole's working on this with me, but he's not here right now. He's still bartending at Seneca's and will be for the next few nights until Omaney leaves the area."

Hunter rose and turned to J.D. "We need to update Jurek on the situation." He looked back at Alex. "And bring Buchanan in as well, before we start stepping all over each other."

"I'll go make a few phone calls. But, Hunter?" J.D. paused when he stepped behind Alex. *Think with your head and not with your dick,* he mouthed with a smirk and disappeared into the bedroom, closing the door behind him.

Hunter glared at J.D.'s retreat. Still, the ass had a point. Hunter was way too aware of Alex in her robe. What was it about finding this woman in various states of undress? He tried to clear the unruly lust from his brain. Where had his professionalism gone? He didn't have time for sex, and especially not with Alex, a woman who rocked the balance he'd strived for years to perfect.

"Care to explain what the hell you thought you were doing?" he asked calmly.

"Want to explain why you thought it necessary to bust into my hotel room?" she answered, just as coolly. She crossed her arms over her chest and regarded him with amusement. "Upset you can't intimidate me? The mighty Hunter Greye not used to being told to kiss off, hmm?"

He zeroed in on her mouth at the word *kiss*. "You know, angel, I could have sworn we already had a conversation about you keeping your pretty little nose out of this."

Fury darkened her face. "You condescending ass. I'm working a case, not playing at being grown-up."

"You're all grown up, all right." He licked his lips, wishing he could put them over her breasts again. Or better yet, venture between those slim thighs for a taste of the woman underneath the anger. He stalked her, pleased when she refused to back away. Hell, he was beginning to really like her. Anyone who didn't shy in the face of his frown demanded respect. "So you thought you could get to Omaney with a little seduction?"

"Why not? It worked on you," she said so sweetly that it took a moment for her statement to process.

"You little witch." He pounced before she could escape, taking her into his arms. "I don't think you remember clearly."

To his shock, she pulled him closer by the collar of his shirt. "No, I'm not mistaken." The sly look in her eyes should have warned him, but his cock wouldn't let him focus on anything but his erection straining to break free.

When she kissed him, it was only natural to return the embrace. Her hands hooked into his shirt, just as her lips softly pressed his, her tongue seeking more. She stroked the nape of his neck, soothing the hungry beast wanting to slake his needs.

Her hands continued to pet him, running through his hair, over his shoulders, and down his chest until he wanted to explode. Her mouth wouldn't let him go, forcing him to deepen the kiss to taste more. The things he wanted to do to her...

He gripped her ass and pulled her closer, grinding against her. When she sighed and nipped his lip, he nearly lost his mind. He smelled her arousal, could sense their energies in line with one another, and knew she was his for the taking.

Until she pushed him back, smoothed down her hair, and raised her eyebrows in question. "You see? I'm not mistaken. Seduction brings the mightiest to their knees every time. Just. Like. That." She snapped her fingers.

To her good fortune, J.D. interrupted them. Because Hunter wanted to grab her by the neck and show her just how things were going to be between them. The urge to claim her shook him, and he took a few minutes to gather his bearings before speaking.

J.D.'s amusement didn't help. "Well, well. Sorry to interrupt...things." He coughed. "Alex has a meeting scheduled with her *agent* at eight a.m. sharp—in our conference room. We'll discuss everything then. Max and Cole will be there too."

"Oh, goodie. A group discussion." Alex sighed.

Male satisfaction replaced his irritation when he noted how hard she was working to regulate her breathing. Her hands shook, but when she saw him looking, she shoved them in the pockets of her robe and glared at him. Good. The little liar wasn't unaffected. Far from it.

Damned if she didn't give as good as she got.

J.D. continued, "After I explained things to Jurek, he agreed that we and Buchanan Investigations need to pool our resources. Apparently, Max agreed. Feel free to call your uncle to confirm it."

"Oh, and, angel? Make sure you're prepared to tell us exactly what happened tonight with Omaney," Hunter growled. "And don't skimp on the details."

J.D. grinned at the hand gesture she shot him.

"Promises, promises," Hunter returned.

She tore past them to the front door and turned around, her robe parting to reveal golden skin and the slopes of two perfect breasts. All in all, a decent way to end what could have been a shitty evening. Even J.D.'s presence couldn't mar the sight of Alex nearly naked.

She pointed at the door. "Get out already. I'm tired."

And frustrated. He had a bead on her now. He walked toward her. "Sweet dreams, angel. We'll look forward to seeing you tomorrow." He kissed her hard and quick, lingering over those soft lips.

"Hell," J.D. muttered.

Alex pushed them out the door and slammed it behind them.

They stood in silence for a moment before J.D. opened his big mouth. "You know you're going to make this joint operation harder to handle by sexing it up with a Buchanan."

"Not a Buchanan, a Sainte," Hunter said with a smile, in a surprisingly good mood considering the mess they'd stepped in. "Don't worry, J.D. I know how to handle her." *One kiss at a time.* "By this time tomorrow, she'll no longer be our worry."

Chapter Five

The next morning, Alex couldn't wait to knock Hunter Greye off his pedestal. Dressed in a conservative pair of slacks and a soft cream sweater, she looked nothing like the vamp from the previous evening. Slipping out the back door of the hotel into a waiting car helped clear her mind. While Cole drove them in a random pattern to shake anyone who might think to trail her, Alex pondered the changes her life seemed to be taking.

No longer the protected younger sister too fragile to get her hands dirty, Alex had successfully acted in her first undercover operation. Though the bottom line remained that she would do everything in her power to save Rebecca, she also felt a liberating sense of empowerment.

I'm finally doing it. Finally a real part of Buchanan Investigations.

Not that information gathering wasn't important, but she grew tired of always sitting back out of harm's way to make Cole and Uncle Max feel better. She couldn't put her finger on it, but sparring with Hunter made her feel just as free. An odd reaction to a man who put her back up, but besting him last night had been a thrill. Until he'd ruined it by kissing her in front of J.D. and reducing her to a puddle of mush. That's all she needed, to be treated like a girl by a strong Westlake type.

And he was strong. She shivered, then tamped down her emotions when Cole suggested turning down the air conditioner. Kissing Hunter Greye was an experience in itself. Dear God, he'd given her an orgasm in her own bathroom. She'd tried hard to pretend it hadn't happened, but she wanted to feel that again.

The dreams she had of them together felt so right. His muscles appealed to her, a controlled strength she found utterly sexy. He knew just how to touch her, how to bring her the most pleasure. She thought about him all the time. She'd be studying the case files and drift into an almost fugue state. Reminded of his eyes, the wild scent of untamable man, or his unyielding power, she dwelled on Hunter Greye, wanting him more and more. None of her confused feelings were rational, and she couldn't stop herself from thinking about him. He haunted her when she should have been focused on this case—her one chance to become a true part of the family business.

Hell, the sexual attraction for the obnoxious man was driving her *crazy*.

Alex couldn't get enough of his lips. That magic mouth, when he used it for anything other than words, brought her nothing but pleasure. She'd never had such an intense orgasm in her life as when he'd touched her in her apartment. And last night, in the hotel room? She'd set out to prove a point, that he couldn't push her around.

She'd proved it, all right. And she'd nearly fallen under her own spell, completely in lust with a man she wasn't sure she liked.

Cole interrupted her thoughts. "I'm doing my best not to ream you a new one for that stunt you pulled last night. What the hell were you thinking, getting in a car with Omaney?"

"Glad to hear you're not going to yell at me," Alex said

dryly.

Cole swore. "Thorne mentioned he did that last night after he tailed you back to the hotel. So I'm trying to be patient with you. Idiot."

"Jerk."

"But you've been sitting there with a really dopey look on your face for several minutes. What's up?" Cole asked, glancing into the rearview mirror as he drove.

She tried to contain her blush. "Drive, Jeeves."

"Nice try."

"Seriously, keep your eyes on the road. We can't afford a crash that'll bring attention to us together."

"Yes, Ms. Tyrell," her brother drawled. "Anything else I can do for you? Want me to carry you inside when we arrive? Some coffee and freshly squeezed orange juice, perhaps?"

"Sure, and throw in a foot rub while you're at it. I hate heels."

Her brother muttered something under his breath she probably didn't want to hear.

"Nothing's wrong. Cole. I'm just excited. My first undercover case and it's working."

"Terrific. Omaney's drooling all over you. I can't wait until he drugs and kidnaps you too."

"Killjoy."

"You know, maybe we'll just finish this drive in silence." He scowled at her in the mirror, and they finished their drive without speaking.

While mentally reviewing her meeting with Omaney and what she planned to say about it at the debriefing, she made a note not to react when she saw Hunter again. Her heartbeat would not race. The butterflies in her stomach would not flutter. And her breathing would remain even, calm. *I'm in charge. I'm the seductress, the actress playing a part. Not a good time for my libido to wake up, and especially not to a man who can't accept a woman with her own strengths.* No way. If she thought Cole overprotective, Hunter would no doubt smother her.

She kept telling herself that as she and Cole arrived at Westlake Enterprises. Like the Buchanan building, this one remained in its own complex away from the downtown area on East Bay Street. Nondescript cars littered the parking garage. The large number of vehicles spoke to Westlake's large agency. While Max owned the Buchanan building, Buchanan Investigations only occupied the top two floors and engaged twenty employees, several of whom worked on a contract basis.

Alex studied the modern decor as they walked to the conference room, curious at the similarities between this walkway and the path to Max's office.

"Weird, huh?" Cole asked in a low voice. Glad to be on the same wavelength with her brother again, she nodded and grinned.

They reached a heavily manned desk and were pointed down another hallway, where they found an empty conference room. A long, oval table with over a dozen chairs dominated the austere space decorated in dark mahogany, plums, and forest greens. A large screen mounted in the ceiling had been pulled down against a far wall, the projector mounted from above.

She and Cole sat just as J.D. entered with Jurek and Hunter, whom she did her best to ignore. On their heels came Max and Thorne.

"What's Thorne doing here?" Alex asked under her breath. She'd thought his part ended last night. After making sure Omaney didn't follow her into her hotel room, he'd given her a piece of his mind—what little he had left. After his lecture, she wasn't sorry to see him go.

"I felt he needed to be here," Max answered. "He's only hired help though, and won't do much more than act as my eyes on this investigation."

Alex watched with amusement as her cousin opened his mouth to speak, then closed it firmly and stared hard at Max. He sighed and plunked down next to her at the table.

Concentrating on Thorne, Alex was able to avoid looking at Hunter. For all of three seconds. Without even trying, Hunter drew her gaze like a magnet. As soon as she looked at him, his eyes met hers. A familiar warmth surged through her at the contact.

"It's time we pooled our resources and worked on this together," Jurek began in a deep voice. J.D. suddenly stood and retrieved a tray of coffee and pastries that had been sitting unnoticed at the rear of the room. "But I'll wait, of course, until J.D. has finished."

J.D. had the good grace to flush as he hurried back to the table, pushing the cart. "Sorry, boss. But it's just after eight and I need something to keep me going."

Alex's stomach chose that moment to grumble.

Jurek turned in her direction. "Obviously you're not the only one." He waited until everyone helped themselves before continuing.

Ah, Java, the stuff of life.

Alex noticed that Hunter passed on everything save a small pastry. He made a face at the coffee. Apparently, Mr. Energy didn't need the jolt like she did. She swallowed the stuff with pleasure, then frowned. She looked into her cup. It tasted like...strawberries?

She peered at Hunter. He stared at the food before him with distaste and suddenly glanced up to meet her gaze. His eyes blazed with anger, and Alex suddenly realized he tasted coffee while she tasted his food.

What the hell is this connection between us?

She blinked in confusion, wanting to distance herself from a truth she didn't know how to face. Her bizarre relationship with Hunter went deeper than she'd thought. She and Cole had a vague awareness of each other at times. Max shared thoughts when she let him in, but nothing more. And certainly nothing so incredibly bizarre as her link to Hunter.

Dammit. Not now. They're just waiting for an opportunity to take this case from me. She was so close to proving herself. She couldn't stop yet. Concentrating fiercely on herself and no one else, she relaxed into her seat.

Her coffee tasted like coffee again, and Hunter turned back to Jurek.

She purposefully ignored her uncle's unnerving stare.

Jurek directed the conversation back to the group. "Finding you Buchanans involved in an undercover role with Omaney sent up more than a few red flags last night, let me tell you. We'd been all ready to move in with a plan when yours put a slight glitch in it. At least, that's what I thought last night." His eyes glowed with excitement.

"But not now," Max added. "Alex's new background fits the profile of the women previously kidnapped. We deliberately baited Omaney, and he swallowed it whole. Our man's not a nibbler."

"New info confirms what we've suspected. Omaney is collecting women for Wraith." Hunter's low voice brushed over Alex like a physical caress.

"Wraith?" Thorne asked.

"A drug runner and arms dealer," Cole explained. "And you're sure this Wraith character is involved? Maybe he's just one of the many criminals Omaney's been linked with."

Hunter shook his head. "Unfortunately, not. We'd planned to use Omaney to get to him. Ultimately, he's the one we want if we ever plan to see Rebecca again."

Jurek nodded. "With the help of Jed Black, we can and will infiltrate Wraith's lair."

"Jed Black?" Cole snorted. "You might as well use Santa Claus to capture Wraith. You honestly expect us to believe you've got a connection with that terrorist?"

Hunter smiled, an expression that warned others to be wary. "You could say that."

Max stared at him intently. "Son of a gun," he murmured. "So Black was never real?"

Cole blinked in surprise. "No shit."

Alex didn't know what the hell they were talking about. She'd never heard of Jed Black, though the description *terrorist* didn't sound promising. Thorne also looked confused, making her feel a little better at being out in the cold.

"Would someone please explain to me what you're all talking about?" she asked.

"Sure thing, angel," Hunter drawled. Max frowned at the dry endearment, but he said nothing. "I'm Jed Black."

"I don't have to remind you that this is extremely confidential," Jurek hastily mentioned, glaring at Hunter. "Next time, warn me when you decide to drop a bombshell around uncleared people."

Max scowled. "Who the hell are we going to tell, Jurek? Colombia? Well, go on. Explain the rest."

"So impatient." Jurek turned to Alex. "Hunter created Jed

Black years ago. A terrorist comes in handy when you need information in far-off places Uncle Sam can't touch. After Hunter left the military, the government continued to build Black's reputation as an arms dealer and smuggler. A man who can be bought for the right price.

"Hunter was the first to use Black's cover, so he's the one to do it again. Black is a tall man with dark hair and dark eyes. He's a nondescript individual, for the most part."

"So how's Hunter going to pull that one off? Nothing nondescript about him. He screams *difficult.*"

"Thanks, Alex." Hunter shot her a rare grin, and to her surprise, she grinned back. "The only real identifier Black has is a scar on his left hand. Cosmetics will give me what I need to get by. With just a few subtle changes, no one will recognize me."

Cole stared at Hunter. "Impressive."

"I would have said scary," Thorne muttered.

"We try," J.D. said around another pastry.

"Small bites, J.D." Jurek rolled his eyes and said something to Max that made him laugh.

Alex studied the individuals across from her. She knew Westlake had a reputation for getting the job done. But she'd never imagined the detailed depths to which they'd go to get their information or their prey.

As if reading her mind, Hunter gave her a knowing look. "Yeah, we have ties to places you can only dream about, so don't think about trying to work around us on this case."

"Hunter," Jurek warned. "I think what Hunter means is that it won't help anyone if we work against each other. Those women out there need our help."

Max nodded. "I agree. We should have been working

together from the start," he reprimanded.

"If it was just up to me, we would have." Jurek sighed.

"And you wonder why I don't like federal involvement." Max shook his head. "So what's the plan?"

"We use your model and our terrorist together," Jurek answered. "We had proposed to send Jed Black to meet Omaney. We've already arranged for a huge arms deal to go down tomorrow night, with Jed in the thick of things. We're hoping to impress Omaney with Jed's money and influence. Our end result will bring us closer to Omaney's boss—Wraith."

"Speaking of Omaney... Alex, tell us about last night," Hunter insisted.

Alex frowned at him before turning to the others. "We have the interaction recorded. I'd say it went well."

"He was on you like white on rice," Thorne said. "The man's hooked but good. Now we reel him in."

Alex nodded.

"Exactly what happened?" Hunter asked again.

A glance at Uncle Max showed him in Hunter's camp. She gave as much detail as she could without getting graphic. "He wanted to spend the night with me. I made up an excuse about an early meeting with my agent."

"That's it?"

Her voice rose. "What's with the interrogation? I'm on your side."

Hunter seemed so intent on her that it took him a moment to realize everyone was staring at him. "What?" he snapped.

"Nothing." Max shook his head when Cole would have spoken. "Alex has a date to meet Omaney and his friend, the owner of the Formati, for lunch."

Jurek rubbed his chin. "You know, with Omaney's interest

so obvious, we could use Alex to smooth Jed's intro. That keeps her safe and the rest of us working together, in the loop. Max? Your thoughts?"

"Instead of falling for Omaney, let's have Alex fall for Jed Black. Alex, Hunter, make sure it's dramatic enough to seem real. Omaney loves a challenge."

"Uncle Max, that's not necessary—"

J.D. interrupted. "Our profile shows Omaney to be a narcissistic ass. He won't like losing Alex. The question is, will he be so intimidated by Jed that he lets her go, or will he take up the challenge? Because we need him to bring Wraith into this."

"Wait a minute," Hunter broke in. "We have an arms deal going down tomorrow night, and I'm going to make off with Alex right before it? That doesn't seem right."

"Good point," Jurek admitted.

Max argued, "Jed's got a reputation as a heavy hitter, so we use it. He can wine and dine Alex while keeping his cool and cementing an illegal arms deal hours later. It's a soap opera gone bad. Do you really think Omaney's going to question Jed's attraction to Alex, considering how quickly *he* seems to have succumbed to her charms?"

Silence filled the room as everyone absorbed the new plan. Hunter turned to her. "How do you feel about this?"

Alex wasn't pleased to once again find herself in the spotlight. She didn't want her family rousing to protect her, the way they always did. And if they thought about what they were asking her to do, they just might.

"I can handle it. I want Rebecca found and Omaney and his partner put away. If you're so sure this Wraith is behind it, then we need to get him off the streets and behind bars where he belongs."

She thought she detected a glint of approval in his eyes before Hunter turned to answer a question from J.D.

A few hours passed while they hashed out specifics and laid the logistical groundwork. Alex needed to return to her hotel. She had a lunch date with the devil.

"Uncle Max? I know you need to straighten things out, but I've got to get back to the hotel. How do you want me to play it with Omaney and his buddy?"

"Just like you have been, Alex. Put Omaney on a tether, but don't pull him too tight. Try to get as much out of Benjamin Anthony as you can. We're not sure how deeply he's involved in this mess, if he is at all."

"And don't worry if you see me wandering around the hotel," J.D. added. "I'm new on the staff and eager to get my hands on Anthony's computer. Gotta love tech support."

She stood, eager to do her part. To her shock, her brother said nothing. Not one peep about his sister going into danger. She didn't want to question her good fortune, but she didn't trust it. Then the other shoe dropped.

Her brother studied Hunter while he spoke to her. "Thorne will drop you back off at the agency. I've got a few things to wrap up here."

Groaning under her breath, Alex left with her cousin. She refused to look at Hunter as she walked out of the room and focused instead on the information she'd learned this morning. But she couldn't help wondering what Cole needed to *wrap up*.

Cole waited until his sister left. "Hunter, I'd like to discuss some specifics of the case with you, privately."

Hunter paused a moment, then nodded. He'd been expecting this. He led Cole down the hall into an empty room and closed the door behind them.

Cole started. "You've played Jed Black before?"

"Yes."

"You apparently do a mean impression of a criminal."

"Yes."

Cole frowned. "Fine. Let's cut the bullshit. Remember that you'll be out there with *my sister*." He approached Hunter until they stood mere inches apart. "Stick to the script and keep your hands off her," he said quietly but with force.

Hunter took a deliberate step back and leaned against the table. He crossed his arms over his chest and studied Alex's brother. They had the same coloring, the same gray-green eyes.

Where Alex possessed feminine features that mesmerized a man, Cole looked surprisingly like his uncle. Though Max's coloring was darker, the expressions on both nephew and uncle were identical. Men looking out for their beloved sister and niece. Hunter sighed. He supposed he couldn't fault Cole's caution. Except that Cole's warning reminded Hunter of his own inability to keep his distance. Though he'd repeatedly told Alex that he didn't screw around on the job, every instinct he possessed told him to take the woman, if for no other reason than to slake this unreasonable lust.

Cole waited for his response, and Hunter had more than a mind to give him one.

"Look, Cole, I'm a professional. If your sister can't keep her hands to herself, well, that's not my problem." The apparent anger on Cole's face warned him he'd struck gold. "Maybe you should be telling her this."

Hunter easily blocked the blow aimed at his face. But he wasn't prepared for Cole's counterstrike, or the way the man clung to his wrist and wouldn't let go.

"Look, Sainte," Hunter growled. "If you want to keep that hand, you'd better let go of me." His anger faded when he noticed Cole's dilating pupils. An invisible psychic miasma filled the room. *Son of a bitch.* Before he could do anything, Cole suddenly let go of him.

"What the hell? Are you all right?"

Cole bent over at the waist, gasping for breath as if he'd just run a marathon.

Hunter reached for him, but Cole jerked back. His eyes slowly returned to normal, and his breathing eased as well.

"I'm fine." He stared at Hunter with a disturbing intensity. "I didn't get much sleep last night," he said lamely. "Must have caught up with me." His voice strengthened as he spoke. "But I'm glad we had this talk." Cole turned unsteadily toward the door. He left Hunter staring after him, baffled.

Another Sainte who made his brain hurt trying to figure him out. He needed to talk to Jurek again. It was high time they got a handle on Buchanan's people. Mind readers, mind manipulators—he thought of Alex—and who knew what Cole was capable of.

The more he thought about Alex, the more he wondered at her game. This morning he'd tasted coffee again. But she'd looked at him askance, as if she'd been startled by the exchange. They needed to set some boundaries before they continued their cover story. He'd be damned if he'd second-guess himself when dealing with Omaney.

As Jed Black, Hunter would need to be firmly in control of everyone and everything around him, including Alexandra Sainte. Sex he could understand. But this constant craving for the woman worried him. Maybe he should do something about it, if only to put his mind at ease.

Yeah, right.

He returned to the main conference room to find J.D. and Jurek talking in low voices, the Buchanans gone.

When he entered, talk ceased.

"Well, how'd it go? Big brother warn you away from his gorgeous sister?" J.D. asked with a smirk.

"It's not funny—" Hunter began.

"Damn right. It sure wasn't funny when you had your tongue down her throat last night."

Jurek frowned. "Is that right?"

"Not a big deal, Jurek. I was just trying to teach Alex a lesson." He shot J.D. a look, promising retribution.

Jurek shook his head. "A lesson? Look, Hunter, Alex is Max's niece. I can promise you that if you mess with her in any way, Max will come at you with both barrels."

"Not to mention what Cole will do," J.D. added, not helping.

"So for your sake and for the sake of this investigation, make sure you play it straight," Jurek warned.

"Yeah, think with your head, not your hormones." J.D. nodded with a straight face.

Hunter's blood boiled as he stared at J.D. Smarmy little—

"Hunter?" Jurek asked with a frown. "You get my meaning?"

"Message received and understood. And totally unnecessary," he growled and turned for the door. "I'll be in my office going over the details. And, J.D., buddy, you're going to get yours. I promise you that."

Chapter Six

Raymond Guest walked to the edge of the bed and ran his perfectly manicured hand over the curve of a milky white thigh. He studied the soft creature staring sightlessly at the mirrored ceiling, a glazed expression on her slack face. He bunched his hands in her long, blonde hair and held tightly for a moment. Then he released his hold and stepped back. What a waste.

He turned and left the room, his feet making little noise on the cool marble floor. As he walked, he peered in the small upper window of each door that he passed, making sure the rest of the occupants of the house slept in reasonable comfort. And health, he thought irritably.

He continued down the stairs and checked on the rest. Six beautiful pieces of flesh, perfect for the little soiree he planned to host in a few days.

He left the building, then walked a small distance back to the main house under a blue sky dotted with puffs of white clouds. Light glistened off the pool to his right, while the dense tropical foliage to his left camouflaged a security fence topped with barbed wire.

He entered his fifteen-thousand-square-foot home with pride, noting the careful attention to detail the staff continued to ensure. Not a thing out of place. Mrs. Simms, God bless her, kept things in perfect order.

Marie Harte

Perhaps he ought to have put *her* in charge of the girls.

Once in the north wing of his home, in what he considered his private quarters, he punched in a security code that he changed daily. Entering his favorite room in the house, he sat with a sigh before his art collection, the one thing in his life that made him truly happy.

Three paintings adorned the wall. Each had been professionally staged, framed, and backlit so that he always had a view into perfection. Yet his eyes strayed, as they always did, to the painting in the middle.

Ray loved the dark and always had. He didn't fear the unknown, the way his bible-thumping parents had. The fine line between life and death fascinated him. The ultimate mystery, a lifeline could be smudged if one wasn't careful. Yet, no matter how many times he looked into the eyes of a person hovering on the brink, he couldn't quite see past that final glaze of shock. The beautiful blonde upstairs had looked empty. No answer to be found there.

Yasef must have given the girl too much Plezure. A hokey name, but his distributors seemed to like it. Plezure had an increased potency over GHB and Rohipnol—other date rape drugs that had glutted the market. Forty milliliters of Plezure could put a hundred-and-thirty-pound woman to sleep. A little bit less made her open to new ideas and suggestions. Too much would put her in a coma and even death.

Apparently someone had used too much, which put Ray in an awkward position. In just nine more days, he would be hosting a party, networking his way into deep pockets. If all went well, he'd appreciate a new foray into the slave market, while expanding his drug enterprise. A man could never be too careful when investing in his future. Wouldn't his parents be so proud?

With a grim smile, Ray paged Yasef and waited.

Though he didn't really trust anyone, he gave his most important tasks to Yasef to complete. Until today, he hadn't been disappointed.

He'd found his assistant years ago in a forgettable little town in South America, sitting in a four-by-four cell. Yasef Cabell had been awaiting execution for a list of crimes impressive in their scope of cruelty. Covered in his own filth, Yasef had stepped forward without a whimper or plea for mercy. He'd remained still, faltering only when a saber removed his pinky finger.

Guerillas had removed two more of his digits before Ray had bought Yasef's freedom. Since that time, the man had never once questioned him or shown the slightest inclination to betray him. If anything, Yasef was better than a pet, a vicious but tamable creature.

A knock sounded at the door. After verifying Yasef's identity via a security feed, he buzzed him inside.

"Yes, Ray? You called?"

"Jennifer has expired," Ray said softly.

Yasef blanched but didn't look away from Ray's displeasure. "She seemed sated when I last saw her. I did only as instructed."

"I take it she needed more than forty milliliters?"

"I started with twenty, but she remained stubborn, so I gradually increased the dose. I think she took fifty before she finally relaxed." Yasef looked wistful. "She did anything I asked without complaint."

Ray knew Yasef had probably used the young woman in ways that no normal man would imagine. But then, wasn't that part of what drew him to Yasef? Such creativity surrounded by madness. Like a twisted mirror of himself.

"Why, then, is she dead?"

Yasef frowned. "I wanted to measure her threshold. She maintained consciousness way past typical dosage. I'm not sure what happened. I'm sorry, Ray."

"I want her disposed of discreetly. Finding a senator's intern raped and brutalized is sure to draw national media attention. And that's something we don't want until well after the fifteenth." He paused. "I don't want a hair harmed on any of the others, or there will be consequences. I'd hate to lose you, Yasef. But sacrifices must be made if we're to be successful."

"Yes, Ray," a subdued Yasef answered. "May I leave now?"

Ray nodded and waited for Yasef to leave, pleased he'd made his point.

When the phone rang, Ray answered it upon the first ring. "Peter, what a pleasant surprise." He smiled into the receiver. "How are things?"

Peter knew what motivated him. They'd grown up together, victims of oppressive fathers and weak-willed mothers. In a place where appearances meant everything, the two had bonded, though their circumstances had been quite different. Peter Omaney, son of wealthy socialites. Raymond Guest, son of an uptight preacher and his miserable, sin-plagued wife.

Neither boy could step a foot out of line without a strap across his back. But perhaps their fathers knew more than they'd thought. Because Ray and Peter now made their lives off other people's sins, and the rewards they reaped would surely see them in hell.

He listened as Peter filled him in on the recent political agenda of a governor he'd been courting. They discussed business for several minutes. Then Peter mentioned his latest conquest, and something in his tone told him this woman had something the others did not.

"What aren't you telling me?" Ray asked.

"You won't believe this, but she's *Corruption*," Peter said with reverence.

Ray froze, his attention drawn to the painting he'd been studying earlier. *Corruption of the Saint* had stood him through both good times and bad. Through the loss of his parents, his sister's tragic demise, and his loneliness over the years when he despaired of ever finding *her*. But now Peter thought she might be the one...

He reminded himself that they had gone this route before. The reason he now had seven—no, six without Jennifer—women waiting in cells to be sold. Even so, he couldn't deny the excitement Peter's words brought.

"I want to meet her. If not sooner, then definitely before the auction."

"I'll make that happen. Trust me, I won't let you down."

Ray hung up the phone and stared at his painting with deep longing. A feminine creature lay sacrificed upon a rock under darkness, under a wraith, he imagined. Under himself. Her image was that of an angel's. But what really mattered most about the woman in the painting was her importance to the darkness. Her white, tattered clothing and wings lay shredded as she surrendered before her dark lord.

He studied the painting and felt a stir of arousal.

Soon, I'll see you soon.

"Ben, this lunch has been absolutely wonderful." Peter included Benjamin Anthony and Alex in his smile. They sat off Benjamin's private office in an intimate setting—Benjamin's private dining area.

A carved mahogany executive desk and leather chair sat before several bookcases, meticulously organized in the attached room. But here, the three of them sat around a large, glass, round table with a marble pedestal. Silk chairs, a crystal chandelier overhead, and Waterford dinnerware with silver-and-gold-veined utensils made her feel like a princess dining with royalty.

The view overlooked the hotel's inner courtyard, which included a large water feature and flowers everywhere. Luxury at its finest. Alex could get used to this.

Ben, as he'd asked to be called, beamed at the compliment. *So far so good.* She drank more of her lemon water, parched due to nervousness or the spicy meal, she couldn't tell. But the way Ben and Peter watched her made her feel distinctly uncomfortable. More than lust tinged their gazes. Speculation and something dark lurked as well. She'd bet her last dollar Benjamin Anthony was dirty.

"So, Ben, tell me again why you won't join us tonight at Seneca's?" She pursed her lips in disappointment and his grin widened.

"I'm too old."

"No way," she denied. "You're Peter's age, aren't you? And I can tell you he's definitely not too old for Seneca's, or anything else," she said suggestively.

Peter blew her a kiss. "You see, Ben? I told you she's magnificent."

"You're right, as usual." Ben glanced at his watch. "Shoot. Peter, Alex, I'm so sorry, but I have a meeting in a few minutes. Please, don't get up. Stay as long as you like." He waved them back to their seats. "If you'll excuse me?"

He leaned down to kiss her, and she forced herself not to

react to the papery whisper of his kiss on her cheek. She watched him leave. An average-looking man, Ben had been a pleasant companion throughout their lunch. He and Peter seemed as thick as thieves, and she wondered if they'd worked together to kidnap Rebecca. She couldn't put her finger on it, but she caught the sense that Ben was involved.

Peter apologized as he glanced at his watch. "I'm sorry, Alex, but I'll have to cry off as well. I've got politicking to do."

Alex pretended a disappointment she didn't feel. God, she was thirsty. Nerves made her sweat, and she prayed Peter couldn't see her discomfort. "I will see you tonight, won't I?" she asked hopefully as they walked out of Ben's private room and into his elevator.

"I think you know I want to see you again." Peter took her hand and kissed her softly on the inside of her palm.

She shivered at the unexpected sensuality of the gesture. Last night, she hadn't felt anything for him but disgust. In the span of one evening and one lunch, nothing had changed. So why did she suddenly want to kiss him back?

"In fact, I want to see *all* of you tonight."

Alex didn't understand the strange look he gave her, but before she could say anything, the elevator doors opened on her floor. Peter escorted her to the door of her suite and waited for her to enter, and then followed her inside and closed the door behind them. Before she could say goodbye, he pulled her into his arms.

At first, Alex didn't mind the kiss. But, as the kiss deepened and turned from pleasant to carnal, her mental alarms sounded. His erection poked into her belly. His cologne nauseated her. She pushed at his shoulders and grew more determined when he reached under her sweater for her breasts. He pinched them and crudely explained what he planned to do

93

to her later that night. Disgusted, Alex shoved Peter from her with her mind as well as her body.

He blinked in surprise. In seconds, all traces of the lust on his face vanished. He looked at her with genuine fondness. "Until tonight, Alex." He winked, turned, and left.

Alex wondered if she'd perhaps imagined the brief attack. But when she touched her tender lips, she knew what he'd done had been real. What the hell had just happened? As she turned around, she felt off-balance. Confused, she didn't know what to think.

Trying to regain her equilibrium, she didn't see Hunter until he stood almost on top of her. "You scared the daylights out of me. What are you doing here?"

Hunter's eyes narrowed. "Nice performance." She blinked, thinking that sounded an awful lot like a sneer. But his blank expression remained in place. "So, what did you get out of lunch, besides a tonsillectomy?" he asked dryly.

"I don't know." She stumbled away from him, barely aware of his hands on her arms to steady her. "The room's spinning." Alex suddenly felt very out of control.

He grabbed her and stared into her eyes. Alex marveled at the rich gold of his irises. Then his pupils dilated, taking in more and more light until his eyes looked black. He breathed deeply, and she smelled...herself.

Her scent wasn't like anything she'd ever experienced. Lavender, the floral scent of her shampoo, and a hint of something utterly feminine that clearly identified her to Hunter. Sidetracked by his gaze, she blurted, "I love your eyes," and once again lost herself in the golden depths.

"Do you?" Hunter sounded distracted.

"Yes... Hey, you breached security and are in my room, *again*," she ended in a huff. Pushing away from him, she managed to find the couch and sat, clutching her head. She felt lightheaded. "Amazing I didn't throw up all over Omaney. What a creep," she complained, then gaped in awe at the genuine grin Hunter threw her way. The gesture made him irresistible.

"Not a good kisser, eh?" He sat next to her, much too close, in her opinion. "So, tell me about lunch."

She suddenly wanted nothing more than to obey. "Benjamin Anthony is in on it. I can't say why, but I feel it. He and Peter are good friends. Ben has a really nice office, and his place serves a terrific meal. The conversation was mild, bland, and uninteresting, really. Still, I felt kind of uncomfortable, as if I were on display or something." She frowned. "In the elevator, Peter kissed my hand. I think I liked it. I must be ill." She felt her forehead, but couldn't tell if she ran a temperature. "But I didn't like him groping me."

"Alex, your eyes don't look right. I think you've been drugged. Tell me again everything Omaney said to you."

She struggled to recall his words and shared them with Hunter.

While she spoke, he put his fingers over the pulse in her neck, startling her with the heat of his touch. She shifted under him, pleased when his fingers dragged over her skin. The buzz in her brain made room for the pure pleasure of his nearness.

She found the energy to knock Hunter onto his back and press him to the cushions by lying flush against him. "Touch me again."

He stared at her in astonishment, but did as she said. His fingers traced a path from her neck to her collarbone, and arousal pierced her, swift and true. Every time they touched, she wanted more. The sheer power underneath his hands aroused her. She could sense his control, and she wanted to see it unleashed, to know she pushed him past the edge of reason.

Marie Harte

He'd brought her to climax so easily, with the taste of his lips and the touch of his hands. She wondered if she could take him past the point of no return as well.

"You know, Hunter," Alex said and licked her lips, aware of Hunter's sudden attention on her mouth. "Omaney doesn't make me feel even a hint of what you do."

He froze, but didn't push her away when she took charge. She put her hands on his chest and started rubbing the soft cloth over his body, grazing his nipples through his shirt. Then she licked at his neck and followed by sucking him gently, leaving small love bites along his skin.

"Oh, God, Alex." His gravelly voice shook her. He put his hands on her shoulders, as if to stop her. But her lips found his, and he pulled her closer.

Alex as the aggressor made Hunter's head spin and his knees weak. Had he not already been splayed out on the couch, he knew his legs would have buckled. Hunter Greye, brought to his knees by a mere female. He tried to sort out his puzzling reaction, but lust overwhelmed him.

Their mouths meshed. He gladly accepted her advances as she explored him. He groaned as her hands lifted his shirt, exposing his skin. Her soft hands felt hot when they rubbed his chest and toyed with his nipples.

He fairly shot off of the couch when she pinched him. And when she bent her head to take his flesh between her teeth, he felt a sudden urge to climax, incredibly ready, *for Alex.*

Knowing he needed to cease, that his sole purpose in visiting her was to stop just this kind of thing from occurring in the future, he nevertheless tortured himself by letting her touch him.

"Alex," he groaned as her lips left him to breathe erotic

96

promises into his ear. "This isn't you. You have to stop," he tried again.

Her body moved sinuously over his, her pelvis riding his erection until he was desperate to fuck her. She thrust her tongue into his ear and ground against him, whispering delights that dragged him into a quagmire of need. She kissed him and shoved her tongue in his mouth, shifting against his cock yet again. And he lost it. Hunter Greye, alpha male, predator, and all around badass, came in his jeans, thanks to a woman too drugged to understand what she was doing.

After his explosive surrender to the inevitable, he caught his breath on her name.

Alex favored him with a sly grin.

"I know you'll want to blame this on whatever they did to me, but it's really you." She placed a soft, stirring kiss on his mouth. "I can feel what you feel and it's driving me crazy," she said, the lust clearly swirling in her dark eyes.

At mention of their connection, Hunter groaned. *Damn it.* She'd done it to him *again*. Though part of him raged that the she-devil had gotten the better of him, he had little to complain about. Because he'd just had the most incredible orgasm he'd ever felt in his life. And for the life of him, he wanted it again, but this time, he wanted her body under his, her acceptance, her surrender.

Shit. This woman is more than dangerous. She's lethal.

To his bewilderment, she apologized. "I'm sorry." She sighed and sat up, wobbling over him. "I didn't mean to take advantage of you." Except *advantage* came out as *avantage*.

Hunter swore, knowing only he was to blame. Alex could barely speak. Was it her fault she was too sexy for her own good? Or his fault he hadn't the strength to resist her? The knowledge that he'd been led by his hormones reminded him of

Anna all over again, and he finally found the strength to pull away.

Gently pulling out from under her, he stood and grimaced at the mess in his pants. *Mission, man. Think of the mission.*

Hunter took a deep breath and exhaled slowly. "This thing, this connection between us, it has to stop."

"Yeah. Cut it out." Alex closed her eyes and snuggled into the couch. She yawned. "I'm really tired."

"Hell." He left and made a phone call requesting help. After getting some sound medical advice from their doctor on staff and a promise of medical attention for the drugged sex kitten on the couch, he returned from the small kitchenette with several bottles of water. "Drink those and then we'll talk."

Three hours later, after cleaning himself up, force-feeding Alex water, and a visit from Westlake's medic on staff, Hunter watched Alex return from another trip to the bathroom. She glared at him.

"I hope you're happy. I just threw up a great meal and have consumed so much water I feel like I'm going to float away."

"Actually I do feel much better, thanks." And not just from that incredible, mind-blowing orgasm. The doctor had confirmed that the drug in Alex's system wasn't lethal. It had a lot of the same similarities found in the recent surge of date rape drugs floating around the club scene. The massive amount of water Hunter had forced Alex to drink, as well as the time between her initial ingestion and now, had gone a long way toward helping her recuperate.

His relief over her recovery struck him as more than simple concern for a colleague. He felt territorial, emotional, and guilty as hell that he'd found pleasure from their encounter when she hadn't. None of it made any sense, and he forced himself to focus on the here and now.

"Well, I think we can now safely assume Omaney wants you any way he can have you."

Alex sighed. "I should have guessed earlier. They served a pretty spicy lunch and kept refilling my water glass. I didn't taste anything odd."

"You wouldn't."

"But I was really thirsty. Had a bad case of dry mouth." She frowned. "Peter Omaney needs to be strung up by his toes."

"I would have said balls, but okay. The asshole is dirty, and so is his buddy. You felt it, right?"

"I did."

Hunter lapsed into silence, but he was completely aware of Alex. Her cheeks looked pink, and he thought her the most beautiful woman he'd ever seen. *Shit, I have got to stop thinking like this.*

"I, ah, I really am sorry I was all over you earlier." Alex cleared her throat. "I was drugged, as you know. But I swear I could feel what you were feeling. It's just so strange."

Hunter nodded, thinking it was past time they had this talk. "Explain this thing you do to me. You've got telepathic abilities, like your uncle?"

Alex shook her head. "Hunter, I keep telling you that I don't know what this connection is between us. For the record, I don't read minds. I've never experienced this...oneness...before with anyone. It's weird, not to mention a little scary."

Hunter wasn't sure what to believe. She sure sounded convincing.

"What can *you* do anyway?" Alex asked, throwing him off balance.

"Hmm?"

"I asked Uncle Max about you. He says that most of you

Westlake guys are psychically gifted."

"Just like you Buchanans and Saintes. You first."

Alex chewed her lip and seemed to come to a decision. She sighed. "Fine." An empty water bottle floated from the table toward his head. It hovered in the air until he reached out and grabbed it.

"Telekinesis," he murmured, intrigued by the possibilities, as well as her obvious discomfort in revealing her ability. "Do you have to see the object to move it?"

"Yes. Now what about you?"

He debated telling her, recalling the mess that had resulted the last time he'd confessed the truth to a woman who'd meant something to him. *Not that Alex means anything to me. Not at all. But we have to work together. We need to trust each other.* And that, more than anything, confirmed his decision.

"I've got enhanced sensitivity," he began slowly. "I'm not psychic. But I can see, hear, taste and smell things with far more acuity than a normal person."

"Wow, really?" She seemed genuinely interested, as opposed to horrified. So far, so good. Hunter had only once before had a conversation like this, and it certainly hadn't been so mundane. He wondered that he didn't feel more exposed for having told her.

"Yeah. When my father was an officer in the Corps, he did some secret missions for the military. He received experimental drugs that he thought were biological deterrents. In any event, nothing happened to my dad. I, however, have this unique ability that enables me to experience life with a degree of clarity that's well beyond a normal person's scope." *Not to mention what Adrian can do.* His brother was just as gifted, and just as secretive about his abilities.

"You're aptly named, *Hunter.*" She didn't seem at all

worried now that she knew the truth.

He kept waiting for her to freak out, as his ex-fiancée had. But she didn't, and something within him eased.

"Is that it?"

"Is what it?" he asked, bemused.

"Is that all you can do?"

"Isn't that enough?" No need to push her further. He didn't plan to divulge his bonus ability—to overtake his prey's mind when he found that perfect pinnacle of connection. A taste of it had pushed Anna out of his arms and out the door for good.

"Fascinating. None of my relatives can do anything so visceral. Mental mumbo-jumbo, but nothing along your lines." She studied him, and he wondered if he could believe the growing attraction between them. Now that the drugs had pushed through her system, he'd expected her to grow wary of him once more. But she didn't. If anything, the woman seemed captivated by his nearness. He was baffled. Women liked him enough in bed. But rarely did they enjoy conversations with him.

Alex rubbed her head. "I guess this odd link we seem to have falls in my court, then. When you first accused me of it, I thought you were crazy. Now it seems it has to be me. You know, I tried to shut you out of my thoughts for a few days last week. Did you have any other weird flashes after our meeting in the coffee shop?"

"No, now that I think about it."

"Probably not until our group conference. I swear my coffee tasted like a strawberry tart. Now that was bizarre."

"Tell me about it."

"I know this is a lot to ask, but I don't want to mention this to my uncle. If he senses there's something wrong with me, he might pull me from this assignment. And I don't want to stop until Rebecca and those women are home safe. I *can't* stop."

"Why?" Hunter took note of her desperation.

"Because I can finally make a real difference. I need to show my family I'm just as capable as Cole. But more than that, I want to help Gina and her husband. I want to give them back their daughter. I miss my mother more than anything. I'll bet Rebecca feels the same."

Hunter might have argued the wisdom of them both continuing the mission with that strange mental business between them. But Alex's sincerity, the depth of pain in her voice when she spoke about her mother, moved him. He knew all about wanting to make family proud. Hell, he could still see his father's broad smile after Jurek's last glowing review. Pleasing the old man had never felt so good.

"Okay. We'll keep this between us for now. If for some reason I sense something you do, I'll just...deal with it."

"Me too." She paused, then blushed bright red. "And, as for before, it won't happen again. I'm sorry I jumped you on the couch. I can't believe I did that."

The scent of her arousal peaked, and the way she avoided his gaze but snuck a glance at his crotch spoke volumes. *The woman still wants me. After everything. Hot damn.*

He gave her a noncommittal grunt, and she frowned. "Don't worry about it, angel. I'll chalk it up to taking one for the team." He grinned at her, and she turned a brighter shade of red. He chuckled, sincerely amused. "Hell, you know what? I'll happily take another one for the team later tonight. Or at least, Jed Black will. He's going to knock you off your feet. So keep that chemistry hot and heavy between us." Control over this entire situation once more settled in his grasp. "And know that no matter what happens, I'll protect you."

"Or maybe I'll protect you," she said softly, her gaze questioning. "You never know."

Chapter Seven

Any night at Seneca's delivered a good time, and Monday night was no exception. Strobe lights blinked and glittered. The music pulsed, and the human masses swaying to the rhythms laughed and danced with abandon. Late summer in the South at its finest.

When Alex walked in the door with Peter, she joined the throng of pleasure-seekers. Before long, she found herself dancing in the crowded section near the DJ. Cole worked the bar and Thorne mingled in the crowd. J.D. had even decided to put in an appearance. No one was taking a chance with her safety. Especially not Hunter, who'd given her so many rules she could barely remember them all.

She forced herself not to look for him. *"You'll know me when you see me,"* he'd said.

Tonight, she wore a sheer black mini dress with strappy black heels. She'd left her hair down, swinging it around her shoulders as she danced, determined to distract Peter for a while.

He'd picked her up in his limo, all smiles. Neither of them mentioned the odd incident in her suite, and he did no more than kiss her lightly on the mouth, though his lips lingered a tad longer than Alex would have liked. He clearly desired her and made no attempt to hide it. He fully expected tonight to end with them having sex; she could feel it.

Over my dead body.

She continued to dance with Peter until he laughingly called a break. A few friends caught his attention as they made for the stairs. Seeing the restroom so close, Alex made an excuse and promised to meet him at his table.

Turning toward the bathroom, she caught Thorne's eye before she walked into the women's lounge and fiddled with her lipstick as she gave herself the extra boost of confidence she needed to be anywhere near Peter after what he'd tried to do. She'd be damned if she'd drink anything he handed her again. The bastard.

She gave herself a few minutes before leaving the lounge. On her way back up the stairs, she deliberately ran into Thorne and dropped her purse. She bent to retrieve it.

"I'm so sorry," he apologized as he knelt to gather the items that spilled from her bag. The crowd flowed around them, giving them a small moment of privacy.

"Everything set?" she whispered.

"Yes." Thorne replaced her lipstick with an identical tube. "Take this. J.D. says it's an undetectable tracking device, just in case you lose your earrings."

Remy had given her the gold hoops in her ears. The earrings served as a constant tab on her whereabouts and gave Max a breath of peace. But having a backup wouldn't hurt.

"Thanks." She smiled at him and would have stood when he grabbed her wrist.

"Not so fast. Give it another ten minutes. See the blonde in the pink dress by the bar? That's my date. Go talk to her. Then, on your way back to Omaney, you'll run into Jed Black."

Alex nodded, but inside she was a bundle of nerves. She

needed to relax. She'd gone over this very plan with Hunter earlier. Time to prove she had what it took for this mission. Thorne made small talk as he pulled her to her feet. He apologized again and left her staring after him.

Alex followed his instructions to the letter. She met up with the blonde and they struck up a conversation under the watchful stares of her bartender brother and Peter, who sat at his table on the second level.

Ten minutes later, Alex left the bar and skirted the crowded dance floor. Before she reached the side stairway, a deep voice stopped her.

"Baby, you look good enough to eat."

She turned slowly to her admirer.

His lips quirked as he assessed her. Tall, with broad shoulders, black hair and dark eyes, he intimidated merely by breathing. A sense of power surrounded him, there in the confident way he moved. He had a bronzed face, no doubt achieved by long hours in the sun. His nose had a small bump in it, as if it had suffered a break. His full lips quirked at her over a square jaw. A familiar jaw.

Holy crap. Was this Hunter?

"And you are?" she asked haughtily, impressed that he'd nearly managed to fool her.

Hunter pulled her back onto the dance floor, in full view of Peter, while people surged around them. His breath whispered over her cheeks, and her body flooded with desire.

"Jed Black, at your service," he mouthed, so close, only a few inches stood between them. He took her hand and kissed her palm, the way Peter had yesterday. Unlike Peter's touch, Jed's lit her up like a Christmas tree. Her nipples hardened and her sex grew moist. Needy. He gripped her hand tighter and rubbed her palm with his thumb. Alex's entire body throbbed.

Good Lord. Talk about taking one for the team.

She stared at Jed in awe. Sex in a bottle and just as mysterious. No one looking at them side by side would think he and Hunter the same man. Jed moved differently. Gone was the stillness so apparent in Hunter Greye. Instead, an almost tangible energy sparked off Jed Black.

He'd done something to the shape of his face and to his nose. Contacts darkened his eyes, and he'd dyed his hair. She couldn't put her finger on any one substantial change that made the men unique from each other. The small things made all the difference.

A glance at his hand didn't reveal a scar, and she tensed. Then he flashed his left hand and she noticed a slash running down his pointer finger and over the base of his thumb that looked quite real.

His gaze stripped her without apology. "He's watching us," he murmured directly into her ear and leaned back again to watch her.

Alex licked her lips, and he followed the movement without blinking. She rubbed her thighs together, wondering if he could smell her need. The intensity in his gaze suggested he could, giving her a thrill that her desire wasn't one-sided.

She had to lean close to talk to him. Between the music and the crowd, the noise level was nearly impossible to talk through. "Okay, I'm ready."

He drew her close and rested his hands on her ass. Alex had to wonder if he was getting into character or having a tease at her expense. Because his every touch made her hotter for more. She looked beyond him to Peter and caught a glimpse of Peter's anger. Then Jed brought her face back to his.

"Give it to me good, angel," he mouthed before his lips found hers.

Alex didn't need to act. The fire of his touch lit her entire body. After a moment of feigned struggle, she surrendered to his embrace. He worked his magic, to the point she nearly forgot she played a part when he slowly pulled away.

Several men whistled and toasted them with bawdy acknowledgement. Jed leaned close and thrust an unmistakable erection against her belly. "Want some more?"

"I, I came here with someone else," she stuttered, remembering her lines. Good Lord, Jed Black was just as bad as Hunter Greye. "My friend Peter."

"By all means, angel. Let's meet him so you can say goodbye."

Jed pulled her with him through the crowd and up the stairwell. The security at the entry to the second floor gave him no problem when he walked by them.

"Alex?" Peter stood, glaring at Jed's hand on hers.

"Peter." She blushed. Jed pulled her close and stroked her back, a proprietary gesture Peter couldn't ignore. "I ran into Jed downstairs. I told him I was with someone, and he wanted to meet you."

Peter studied Jed before smiling politely. He motioned to his table. "Please, won't you join us, Mister...?"

"Jed Black." Jed smiled, showing straight, even teeth.

Peter blinked, seeming taken aback at the introduction. "It's a pleasure to meet you, Jed." He glanced from Jed to her and back again. "So, how do you know Alex?"

"I don't, not yet." Jed's gaze roamed her figure, settling disconcertingly on her breasts before he met Peter's stare. "I saw her downstairs and knew I had to meet her."

"Ah. Please, sit down. What brings you to town, Jed?"

"Business." Jed smiled coolly at Peter as he and Alex

settled into their chairs. "Have we met before? You look familiar."

Alex watched the scene unfold as both men tested each other.

"I own several businesses in the area," Peter said as he sipped his drink. "My picture is often in the paper for one political rally or another. In fact, just last week, I hosted the city's annual Justice Ball."

"Justice Ball? So, you're a lawman? Not exactly my thing. I'm a private entrepreneur." Jed changed the subject. "So, you and Alex are friends?"

"Yes, we are," Peter answered quickly. He picked up Alex's hand and kissed it, right where Jed's mouth had been.

Alex allowed her discomfort to show with a hesitant smile and a glance between the men. She wanted Peter to see her as unsure, confused. She'd arrived with Peter, but Jed's pursuit made an impact. Now to show Peter without being too obvious.

"Good friends?" Jed asked with a hint of disbelief. "What do you say, Alex? You fucking him?"

Alex didn't have to fake her discomfort this time. "I only met Peter a few nights ago. But he's very sweet, and we did arrive together here tonight."

Peter's satisfied grin told her she'd pleased him.

But Jed wasn't finished. "Alex, honey, I wasn't finished our dance."

"Well, I don't know." She paused with a quick glance at Peter's face.

Jed pulled out a wad of cash and handed her a hundred dollar bill. "Go get yourself another drink, and I'll join you in a minute."

Unable to deny the command in his voice, she complied

with an apologetic look at Peter. She left, hoping she'd done her part. Now it was up to Jed.

The minute her feet hit the stairs, Jed turned to Peter with a shark-like grin. "Okay, Peter. Let's lay it on the line. Alex wants me. I'm leaving here with her, and there's not a whole lot you can do to stop me. I always get what I want," he added with just enough arrogance to make Omaney clench his jaw.

The asshole regarded him with narrowed eyes. "Is that so?" He rubbed his fingers over the condensation on his glass. "You mentioned you're here on business. I might be able to help you. I'm an important man around here, one who has connections. For example, say you needed extra security around the docks tonight. I could make sure the police arrived in record numbers to provide assistance."

Perfect. Omaney had already heard and swallowed the rumors floating around about Jed Black's business with the Cortez brothers. The man's grim smile and loosely veiled threat said much about his growing attachment to Alex. She'd gotten under the man's skin faster than they might have hoped. Hunter wasn't surprised.

"You know, Pete," Jed said, his trademark ego intact. "I know a few folks in the federal department who are really interested in your ties to Wraith."

Peter didn't so much as blink, though his hand tightened around his glass.

Hunter shrugged. "I figure they're on a wild goose chase. But I hear things. I know someone is moving a very precious commodity pretty soon. A beautiful, living and breathing commodity worth a lot more than that wonder drug your nonexistent friend is peddling."

Peter merely stared at Jed, neither confirming nor denying

anything.

"I think it might prove fruitful for us to do business. Now, the way I figure it, I've got something you want." He tapped his finger against the glass table.

"And what would that be?"

"Besides my contacts and my information? The girl, Peter. I've got Alex in the palm of my hand, and soon enough in my bed. But I'm not a greedy man. You arrange for a meeting with your *friend*, and I'll deliver the woman as a token of good faith."

Peter seemed to mull the idea. "What makes you so sure she's worth it?"

Interesting he didn't deny Jed's claim on her. "Well, she's worth a hell of a lot more than Rebecca Mitchell."

Peter's energy flared, the scent of fear ripe in the air. "Who?"

Got you, you bastard. "I know, Peter. But you don't. You have no idea what I'm capable of. I'll be moving millions in arms tonight, right under the nose of the Feds and the police. They can't touch me. And neither can you," he said in a low voice and stood. He tossed Omaney a business card with a cell phone number scrolled across it. "Set up a meet. I want what your partner has to offer. Screw me over and I'll slit your throat, no questions asked."

He turned to leave when Peter stood.

"Jed, wait."

Hunter turned and noted the open frustration on the man's face. Jed Black's reputation put the fear of God into those who crossed his path. Omaney was no exception.

"I'll see what I can do about my...friend. Just don't harm the girl. She's worth more than you know." Peter frowned, clearly not happy about losing.

"Don't sweat it. She won't have a mark on her. Tell me, is she as good as she looks?" he asked.

"Better," Peter murmured, his attention riveted to Alex below, standing by the bar. "If you're serious about a meet and greet, you're going to have to take good care of her. And I'm going to need some proof that you really are who you say you are."

"Be at the docks tonight. You'll see plenty." Hunter nodded and left. He found Alex surrounded by several men while her brother kept a subtle watch over her.

"It worked," he whispered and nipped at her earlobe. In a louder voice, he ordered her to accompany him to the dance floor, sure Omaney watched it all.

In the middle of the crowd, he commanded space. Going on instinct, he ran his hands over Alex's curvy frame, resting his hands over her taut ass as he pulled her into his growing erection. The excitement of his triumph over Omaney was enhanced by Alex's arousing presence.

Though he knew they played a part, his body couldn't tell the difference between reality and fantasy. He felt every press of her breasts against his chest and could smell her essence with a dizzying familiarity as his body urged him to move even closer.

Jed wouldn't ask. Jed would take. That in mind, *Jed* yanked her head close for a kiss. He kissed her breathless and thought she was doing a hell of a job playing her part. His dick rode her crotch, fitting perfectly against curves made just for him. Her breasts fit his palms, and he made no pretense about the fact he was sexing her up in the middle of a crowded dance floor.

Before he forgot he played a part, Jed raised his head and caught Omaney's fierce gaze. He gave Omaney a nod, his job done, and decided to end this part of the evening. Escorting her away from the jeering crowd and out a back exit, he pulled her toward the car waiting for them. Hunter made sure to give anyone still watching a picture to remember. He ravaged Alex's mouth and neck, wrapping her leg around his back as he surged against her core, wanting nothing more than to finally thrust deep inside her.

It took J.D. clearing his throat for the third time before Hunter let her go.

Hunter gave him Jed's grin before entering the limo with Alex in tow. Once they sped away from the club, Alex shot across to the seat facing him and sat back on the cushions, panting for breath.

"I swear, Hunter, if you grab me one more time, I'm going to belt you." She glared at him over heaving breasts and a sweet perfume that spoke of her need as clearly as the lust in her emerald gaze.

"Really?" he said smoothly. "Because it sure didn't seem like you were putting up any resistance. Oh, that's right," he mocked. "You were acting, weren't you?"

Prodding Alex's temper eased his own frustration with tonight's performance. Or lack of performance. He shifted uncomfortably in his seat.

J.D. lowered the window separating them and grinned into the rearview mirror. "You guys are making me sweat and Cole swear. Nice work. So, tell me, how do you think it went?"

Hunter shrugged. "Omaney's familiar with Black's reputation. He didn't put up a fight for Alex, though he wanted to. He'll convey to Wraith everything I told him. I mentioned Rebecca's name. He knows that I know."

Alex frowned. "Was that wise?"

"I needed to impress upon your playboy that Jed Black

113

knows all, sees all, and is not a man to be trifled with. And then I delivered the killing blow. I took his woman."

"Great. So now we go back to the Formati to reinforce the idea we're together?"

"I'll stay with you for an hour or so, then leave to do business on the docks. I'll return to your suite to get you around five. Be packed and ready to go."

When they stopped at the hotel, J.D. once again played the role of chauffer. As he stood holding the door for them, Alex leaned close to tease him.

"You really do wonders for the uniform."

Before J.D. could say anything, Jed knocked him back as he exited the limo. He tucked her under his arm as they walked to the elevator together, acting extremely possessive as he ran his hand over her hip. He drew soft circles over her thin dress, and Alex had to grit her teeth not to moan aloud at the exquisite sensation.

I'm playing the role of his lover. This isn't real.

They entered the elevator and she forced herself to take a step back, needing the small space for self-preservation.

Thankfully, they rode alone. But Hunter left nothing to chance. He leaned closer to her and whispered, "There's a camera on us. Play to it." He nipped her ear and enveloped her in his solid arms. When he kissed her, he blazed a trail over her lips and down her neck.

Thoughts of their deception fled as his hands rose from her waist to cover her breasts, his fingers passing over her aroused nipples again and again, until she wanted to beg him to take her.

Alex groaned, her head thrown back as he sucked at the

column of her throat.

"Oh, yeah, baby," he said huskily as his gaze rose to meet hers. The elevator stopped. When the doors opened, he pulled her down the hallway, past several astounded couples.

Alex's sanity returned as she realized how she must have looked. Flushed and mauled by Jed Black. Hell, she'd let the man fondle her in the elevator, *on camera*, for the enemy to see.

God willing, her family would never see that video. Cole would have an absolute fit if he saw how far she and Hunter had gone to be convincing.

Hunter could say what he wanted, but their act felt very real to her, as did the proof of his arousal when it dug into her hip. If things continued to grow more intense than their scene in the elevator, she feared they'd become lovers in truth. And considering they'd both experienced orgasmic pleasure in each other's arms, there wasn't much point in lying to herself. Alex desired Hunter Greye, plain and simple.

As she waited for him to unlock her door, she didn't know how she felt about her craving. On the one hand, she didn't view Westlake as the enemy anymore. She still considered them competitors, but having gotten to know J.D. and Hunter better, she didn't see them as the evil scourge of government yes-men she'd once thought.

Yet, her very real desire for Hunter unnerved her. Some part of her wanted to surrender to him, fully accepting his dominance. Half the time she wasn't sure she liked him, so why did wrapping her legs around his waist and holding on while he took her feel so right? Hell, just thinking about his *lips* made her hot. They obviously had the right body chemistry. That still didn't explain their *connection* though, that sense of oneness she'd only ever experienced with him.

Hunter held the door open for her. She entered, tensely

waiting for him to make another move. When he didn't, she let out the breath she'd been holding. He gave her a wide berth and entered the kitchenette.

Grabbing a bottle of water, he chugged it down in one large swallow. He approached the couch with a sigh and lay on it, his six-four frame hanging over both arms of the sofa. Then he fiddled with his watch.

"Hunter?"

"Give me an hour," he muttered and closed his eyes. In seconds, his breathing evened. Amazingly, the man had fallen asleep.

At rest, he definitely looked like someone else. The cosmetics were amazing in their ability to reshape his looks. Hunter seemed almost soft, his bronzed face relaxed. His breathing gradually deepened as she watched.

Irritated that she still wanted him when he couldn't care less, she stomped into her bedroom to change clothes. She put on a pair of silk pajamas—a long-sleeved top and boxer set that her cousin Storm had given her last year on her birthday. She couldn't see anything revealing with her outfit. No way he could accuse her of trying to seduce anyone in this thing.

As if Hunter would care. She couldn't believe he'd fallen asleep. They should have discussed tonight's strategy and whether or not it needed tweaking. Not that she could survive any more *tweaking* without screaming her release to the high heavens. She'd had to change out of wet panties, for God's sake. *Just an adrenaline rush that I shouldn't confuse for sexual attraction. Nothing more than that. If a veteran like Hunter can deal with it, so can I.*

She slipped into bed. The minute she fell onto the satin sheets, she felt an immediate exhaustion. Too much stress, she thought, and snuggled with her pillow. Alex fell asleep trying to convince herself that her partnership with Hunter would remain platonic. They had a case to solve, period. No sense in longing for what couldn't—shouldn't—be.

Hunter breathed a quiet sigh of relief the minute he heard Alex step away and close the door to her bedroom. The water he'd guzzled hadn't helped to cool him off, so he'd found sanctuary in playing possum.

He wondered what she thought when she looked upon Jed Black's features. Personally, he thought Black would appeal to her better than Hunter ever could. His alter ego had a brutal but sophisticated presence that someone like his friend Rafe or even J.D. looked at home with. Hunter always considered himself coarse, not like a polished criminal who could have stepped off the cover of a magazine.

As he lay awake, he tried to concentrate on the case instead of every sound and scent from Alex's bedroom. The whisper of silk over her body as she'd redressed tempted him like crazy to say the hell with their assignment. He needed badly to sate his aching desire. The thought of doing so was enough to ruin what little peace he'd managed.

Knowing he'd never get rest without easing himself, he pulled a handkerchief from his back pocket, then unzipped his pants and reached inside. His cock was steel hard, needing to come in the hot woman just a few feet away. Imagining how good her pussy would feel gloving him, Hunter began stroking himself, not surprised at how quickly his hunger flared. Rocking against her, feeling her breasts over his chest on the dance floor and touching the bare skin of her back, had about killed him.

Alex was so fucking beautiful, so sexy, she made him ache. His cock was so thick, so hard. He needed to come. In her pussy, her ass, God, her mouth.

He could all too clearly envision her on her knees, servicing him. His sexual slave, sucking him deeper as he pushed himself to the back of her throat...

Hunter bit back a groan as he came hard into the handkerchief, wishing he were jetting into Alex instead. It took him a few moments to come down, but the sexual ache no longer distracted him from sleep.

He righted himself before moving to the bathroom to clean up. After disposing of the mess he'd made in the trash, he walked back into the suite, drew the heavy drapes and extinguished all the lights. Then he moved to the couch and lay down.

Cursing his acute senses, he willed himself to relax. Time passed. Just as his body settled down, someone knocked at the door. He sighed and sat up.

The door opened slowly, and J.D. entered. Anyone coming into the suite would be in complete darkness, while Hunter could see just fine. He watched J.D. walk cautiously into the room after relocking the door behind him.

"Welcome," Hunter said dryly.

J.D. jumped and swore. "Thanks for scaring me to death," J.D. snapped. "It's time. You ready?"

Hunter nodded, then realized J.D. couldn't see him. "Let me check on Alex before I go. You're going to keep an eye on her until I get back, right?"

"Yeah, yeah. I highly doubt Omaney's going to try anything after you put your mark on her, but on the off chance he does, I'll be here. I guess it won't look too awkward if your chauffer plays bodyguard while you're out selling illegal arms." J.D. sighed. "Go ahead. We'll be fine."

Hunter didn't like J.D. using the word *we* in context with Alex. Irrational as he knew the feeling to be, he couldn't help the niggle of jealousy that ate at him at thoughts of Alex in J.D.'s company, alone in a hotel room.

He swore to himself and hurried into the woman's bedroom. She lay on her stomach, her golden hair blanketing most of her face except for her eyes. Long lashes covered her cheeks like smudges of charcoal, hiding the contradictory innocence and sexiness that continued to captivate him.

Helpless to stop himself, he ran a finger over her cheek. She sighed in her sleep and rolled onto her back. Her covers fell to her waist, and Hunter gritted his teeth in frustration. A few of the buttons of her shirt had come undone, leaving the swells of her breasts visible.

Annoyed that J.D. could have easily seen her in such disarray, Hunter buttoned up her shirt and dragged the covers up to her neck. She frowned in her sleep, but didn't move.

"Good," he whispered harshly. "You shouldn't be so exposed anyway. You never know who might be walking in that door."

She still didn't stir, and Hunter realized he'd been hoping to wake her, if only to see that look in her eyes when she watched him, that desire she couldn't quite bank.

Cursing himself for a fool, he strode from her room and drove himself to the docks. Jed Black had a reputation to maintain.

Jed finished his business with Ramon and Diego Cortez. They laughed and joked in Spanish and promised to continue business with him, only next time in Miami, where they had a new line of work coming through.

He watched them leave by boat with a look of satisfaction on his face. He didn't turn when Omaney showed on the dock, three unmarked police cars behind him. He'd known they'd arrived, had heard them as soon as they'd gotten within a quarter mile of his exchange. Jurek had a team already waiting to quietly clear out the cops.

Hunter waited for Omaney to approach him. The police waited in their vehicles some distance away. A show of strength, no more, and one that would mysteriously disappear before Omaney left for the night.

"Good work when you can get it, eh?" Omaney asked, his dark hair blowing in the wind, his blue eyes shining under the light of the moon.

"Sure is." Hunter grinned with Jed's conceit.

"I'm impressed by how efficiently you do business. You seem to have quite a reputation as a man no one can seem to pin down, Jed. I wonder why that is?"

"Because I don't leave witnesses," Hunter growled with menace and watched as Peter's eyes shifted nervously around him.

Hunter followed Omaney's gaze and stilled when he saw a figure crouched in the shadows by his own vehicle, a man who would have been impossible to see without Hunter's acute vision. The silhouette showed a pistol by the man's side.

Hunter deliberately turned to smile at Omaney, the threat present in the smile that didn't reach his eyes. He had to move fast. "So, you think to threaten me out here with all of your police for protection? Your friend doesn't look too troubled at the idea of making war with Jed Black." The clouds shifted overhead, spearing a light over the lone intruder by Hunter's car. The bastard raised his gun and sighted in on Hunter.

Peter noted the man with surprise and he answered quietly, warily, "That's not my guy."

Hunter turned and shot the man in a blur. No Westlake agent or policeman would be out on these docks without clearance from Jurek, which he wouldn't have given without informing Hunter first.

Peter stared at Hunter with new respect. "Nicely done. But now you've got witnesses."

"Do I?" Hunter asked quietly.

Peter turned and suddenly found that his police escort had vanished. The cars remained; the individuals in them had gone. He swallowed audibly and tried to charm his way out of danger.

"Oh yes, Jed. You're very impressive."

"You know why you're still alive, Peter?" Hunter asked.

Peter shook his head. He didn't betray himself with a show of emotion, but Hunter smelled the man's fear.

"Because I want to meet Wraith. He's the only thing saving your ass right now," Hunter explained.

Peter nodded. "I've spoken to my friend. Contingent upon tonight's success, he wanted to meet you. You seem to be as much a legend as he is. I have your number. We'll be in touch, so don't make plans to go far in the next two weeks. That prospective auction will soon be arriving. Alex will be all the invitation you need to arrive."

Hunter grinned. "Not a problem. I have her, and I'll continue to have her all week long. She's so fucking sweet, Pete. Who knows? Maybe I'll decide to keep her if she pleases me as much as she did tonight."

He couldn't miss Peter's look of dismay.

"So, is this goodbye, then?" Hunter asked.

"Oh no. I wouldn't dream of missing the meeting of Jed

Black and Wraith. I'll be at the auction; you can count on it."
Omaney nodded and turned in the direction of the police cars.
He entered one of them and drove away.

Cocky bastard.

Hunter hurried back to his car, more than curious about
the man who'd planned to kill him. Once by his car, he was
surprised to see one of the underground's paid assassins, Luke
Romero, who stared sightlessly up at him.

Hunter didn't believe Omaney had hired Romero. The
man's surprise had been too genuine. Perhaps Wraith had hired
him? But that didn't make sense either. No one Stateside had a
grievance with Jed Black, and Jed hadn't been in town long
enough to earn the attention of those who could have put out a
major hit like this. So who the hell had hired Romero?

Chapter Eight

Alex sighed with pleasure as hot water streamed over her body. She hated mornings, and this one felt earlier than others. But at least she could enjoy a relaxing shower in peace.

Afterward, she dressed in a pair of unassuming jeans and a soft cotton blouse and tied her hair back. When she exited the bedroom, she saw a tangled blanket on one of the couches and frowned.

Had Hunter already returned? The smell of coffee negated the thought, since Hunter had made it a point to tell her how much he hated the stuff. J.D. stood, half dressed in the trousers he'd worn last night, looking rumpled and wholly male as he yawned over the brewing pot.

"Good morning." Alex grinned at the tousle-haired blond.

"Morning," he replied. "My, don't you look pretty?"

"I should say the same. What are you doing here?"

"Maybe I just like you?" At her snort, he sighed. "Hunter wanted me to sit with you while he worked his deal. He should be here soon." He scratched absently at his washboard of a stomach.

Alex followed the movement with approval. If she had to be stuck with someone, at least he was a dream to look at.

"Nice abs." She quirked a grin when he suddenly flexed

before her. "And nice arms."

He winked and poured her a cup of coffee. "I've been working out."

He didn't have the bulk of muscle that Hunter did, but J.D. had an athlete's body and model-handsome looks to go with it.

"What exactly do you do for Westlake, J.D.?" Alex asked, taking advantage of a perfect opportunity to ferret information on Westlake Enterprises, or better yet, on Hunter.

"Who, me? I'm a lowly IT rep trying to make his way into the big, bad world of operations. I've only been a field agent for the past year. Before that, they shoved me in the research department, in a cubicle far away from people."

She knew the feeling. "Do you like field work?"

"Well, it's not boring, I'll give you that." He studied her, and Alex had a sense of J.D.'s particular brand of danger. He didn't brood like Hunter. J.D. had a keen intelligence and an ease of manner that urged trust. A powerful one-two combination on top of his good looks.

"What about Hunter?" she found herself asking and could have kicked herself when J.D. smirked. "How long has he been with Westlake?"

"Hunter? Hmm, let's see. I started ten years ago. Rafe followed a few years after me. Hunter? I think he's been with us four or five years now."

"Who's Rafe?" Alex asked. She hadn't yet met him.

"Rafe's another heavy-hitter at Westlake. He's on a case right now or he'd be in the thick of this one. He, Hunter, and I tend to irritate Jurek on equal levels."

Alex laughed. "I know what that's like. I always seem to be apologizing for something I've done to irritate my uncle. Cole's the good one."

"I find that hard to believe." J.D. shook his head. "What about Thorne? Where does he fit in?"

"Thorne's my cousin, one of three on the Buchanan side. He's the oldest. Luc's his brother, Storm his younger sister. Trust me, Thorne's just as bossy as Cole."

"Lucky you."

"And none of them can make coffee." Alex sighed as she took another sip from her cup. "This is heavenly, J.D. I might just have to take you back with me when this is over."

"Oh, really?" a dry voice interrupted them.

Alex shot a startled look at Jed Black.

"I didn't hear you come in." J.D. frowned.

"I know." Hunter slammed the door shut behind him and carried his duffle past them into the bedroom. He slammed her door too.

"What a grouch," Alex mumbled. A glance at J.D. showed him trying to hide a smile. "What's so funny?"

"Nothing. You know, Alex, Hunter's a very interesting individual," he said and leaned over the counter, increasing the intimacy between them.

"Oh?" She looked behind her at the closed door.

"He worked for the government for a long time. But since he's been with Westlake, I've rarely seen him lighten up about much. He's a pretty intense guy."

"I've noticed." She grimaced.

"But he's on the level," J.D. hurried to add. "He might not pour on the charm, but he doesn't play games. If Hunter tells you something, it's as good as gold. There's no one else I'd rather have at my back," he said seriously and glanced over her shoulder before looking back at her. "Alex, you're a gorgeous woman. But there's a lot more to you than looks. Hunter's not so steady around you. Not like he is with other women."

She frowned, not liking the sound of that. "Um, thanks?"

"Tell me something. You like him, don't you? I see you watching him. You look at him the same way he looks at you."

"You sure that's coffee you're drinking and not booze?" She tried to lighten the mood. What did J.D. expect her to say? That she couldn't get the arrogant Hunter Greye out of her mind? That as much as he made her want to pull her hair out, he intrigued her on a deeper level? That she wanted to get to know him as a person, a friend, and God help her, a lover?

They chitchatted about other things for a few minutes. Alex was relieved that she no longer had to deal with J.D.'s obvious matchmaking.

J.D. set down his cup and walked around the counter to her. "Would you do me a favor, Alex?"

"It depends."

His grin should have reassured her, but it didn't. "Nothing illegal, nothing kinky." He glanced over his shoulder again, then faced her and cupped her cheek. "Let me kiss you, just once." He slowly lowered his mouth.

Curious to his motives, Alex waited. She hadn't felt any vibes from J.D. that he desired her before now. And his constant glances at the bedroom door told her he did this for someone else's benefit. What exactly did he think would happen? And why was she suddenly dying to know as well?

The kiss stirred warmth, comfort, but no melting desire. Nothing on the scale of Hunter's touch. No sooner did his kiss begin to deepen when she found herself standing alone. J.D. struggled for air as Jed Black held him pinned to the wall, his hands wrapped around J.D.'s throat.

"Hunter? What the hell are you doing?" Alex asked in

shock.

"A great question I should be asking you two," he growled before releasing J.D.

The idiot coughed on laughter as he tried to regain his breath. "See?" he rasped to Alex.

"See what? That Hunter has homicidal tendencies?"

"I ought to pound some sense into that thick skull of yours," Hunter said coldly to J.D. Then he turned on Alex. "And what do you think you're doing? Seducing J.D. isn't going to solve anything."

"Seducing J.D.?" she repeated, incredulous. "Hunter, it was a harmless little kiss."

"Harmless?" J.D. sounded insulted.

Hunter ran his hand through his hair with frustration, his features stark and cold, the essence of Jed Black, or was that Hunter Greye? The light gold in his eyes hid under dark contacts that turned Jed's angry stare black. To her bemusement, his frustration and anger bled into her. Alex didn't understand it, but she felt Hunter's jealousy as if it were her own. The knowledge secretly thrilled her, until he opened his mouth again.

"If you two want to play footsie with each other, do it later. I've told you before that we can't afford distractions right now." Hunter glared at Alex. "And you should have had all the pawing you can take, or wasn't last night enough?"

She poked him in the chest, fuming at the both of them.

"You're damned right I'm tired of being mauled. This is a job, like any other. And if you can't handle that..." She paused to poke him again, "...then maybe you should ask to be reassigned."

That said, she stormed to the bedroom to collect her things.

J.D. coughed weakly before he straightened up. "If you could have seen the absolute look of rage on your face. Talk about drowning in a sea of green."

Hunter swore. "Let it go, J.D." He walked to the window and stared through the sheer curtain at what promised to be a sunny day.

He felt like an absolute fool. So much for professional behavior. But what did he expect? He hadn't slept in over thirty-six hours, and constant reminders of Alexandra Sainte wherever he stepped didn't help.

The shower should have been soothing, but her scent had lingered in the stall, a sweet lavender that turned him rock hard and roaring to have her.

After he'd emerged from the shower, already on edge, the sight of J.D. plastered to Alex knocked him off balance. An instinctive need to possess and claim had taken over. To Hunter's shame, he wasn't sorry Alex had seen it. Did the woman not understand that, until this case ended, he was responsible for her? Until they settled things between them, she belonged to him and him alone.

He groaned aloud as his words registered. *Belonged to him?* So much for objectivity. This case had been different from the get-go. Women kidnapped from prominent families. The involvement of Buchanan Investigations and Alexandra Sainte. Moving parts that made little sense except when put in the proper context—Alex lying in Hunter's arms. *Now what the hell do I do about this fixation?*

J.D. slapped him on the back, then retreated at the scowl Hunter gave him. "Now, now. I'm sure she'll forgive you. I mean, it really is unprofessional of you to drool over your Buchanan date, not to mention nearly choking your partner. But I can see where you'd find her distracting. Just make sure to name your firstborn J.D. and we'll call it even."

"Shit. I'm going to put my fist through your face, and we'll see how you like—" Hunter would have lunged forward, but Alex interrupted by walking back into the room.

Her displeasure with the two of them was readily apparent. Still, Hunter took comfort in the fact that she ignored J.D. as he threw on his shirt and shoes.

"Think we can all behave like adults?" she asked, tossing her head so that her hair fell in waves over her shoulders.

Adults? He'd be more than happy to show her just how *adult* he could be. His fingers itched to slide through that golden hair, to pull her close and capture that ripe mouth until he was good and done with it. He'd pinch those tight nipples before he took them between his lips. Then he'd shove his cock hard and deep into her hot pussy. He—

She tossed her bag at him, which he caught with ease, and waited to leave. Just then his cell phone rang.

He answered it. "Yeah? Good. We'll be there," he said before hanging up. He turned to J.D. "Take the car and meet us out back. Thorne's verified we're clear. Call us when you're ready."

J.D. shot him a one-finger salute before leaving, once again attired as a chauffer.

Alex crossed her arms and glared at him. He let the silence build, needing to avoid another argument. With his luck, he'd end up dropping his guard and making love to her on the couch. Not the best way to appear in control and in charge on this mission.

To his relief, J.D. soon called. They took the elevator down silently and left as quietly through the back exit into their waiting limo. As J.D. drove them to the drop-off where they would switch cars and head back to their respective headquarters, Hunter couldn't help wondering where to go from here.

The miles passed in silence, giving Hunter time to consider Alex's part in all this. There were more holes in this plan than he wanted to contemplate. Omaney expected him to bring Alex to the auction—the last place she needed to be. Hunter would have his hands full trying to find and free Rebecca. He couldn't keep an eye on Alex and do his job, not unless he trusted her. And he couldn't—didn't.

Then there was that matter of the attempted hit on him last night. If Omaney really didn't own Romero, then who had put out the contract on Jed Black? Jurek was investigating, but Hunter had a bad feeling in the pit of his gut. He really could have used Rafe's help on this one, but with Rafe working on something big for Jurek, he'd have to deal with this on his own.

At least he'd cemented Jed's reputation. Last night had earned him bonus points with Omaney. He'd sold several million dollars worth of small arms and assault rifles, once confiscated by the U.S. government and subsequently tagged, to known drug suppliers while the police charged an empty, run-down warehouse. Proof that Jed could handle the police and shifty deals with drug runners. Or course, unbeknownst to the Cortez brothers, distribution of those weapons would lead to future arrests under the government's watchful eye.

Alex shifted in her seat, drawing his attention all too easily. In jeans and a pink shirt, she looked innocent and pure. And good enough to eat.

"You going to sulk the whole way there, princess?" he asked her to break up the quiet.

She pursed her lips and kept her gaze on the window.

Shit, she looks just as sexy in profile. I am totally screwed. If only Hunter could get rid of his feelings for Alex as easily as he'd handled last night. His attraction for her went deeper than the physical, which puzzled him. Because he wanted more from her than sex. He wanted to know what she liked and disliked. He was curious about her work with Buchanan Investigations. And he wanted to know what she'd think about him if she knew what he could really do.

Opening himself up to Anna had been a huge mistake. His fiancée, the woman he'd thought he'd spend the rest of his life with, had feared and eventually rejected him. They'd been engaged for two years. He'd known her better than he'd ever known another lover. And still, he'd hesitated to share everything. His mother had been adamant. *"If you're going to give your life to this woman, then make it honest. Tell her the whole truth."*

Yeah, well, Mom didn't know everything. He'd told Anna all of it, even showed her the monster that lived within. And she'd bolted.

Now he had intense feelings for another woman, and everything about the situation had *wrong* written all over it. They currently worked together, undercover. Her family had a habit of breaking the law when it suited them, which went against the black-and-white principles ingrained in Hunter since birth. He didn't really know her. But worst of all, Alex made him lose his focus without even trying.

Physically, they fit. As if she'd been made for him, when together, her body rested against his like pieces of a puzzle that clicked into place. And her telekinesis made her as big an oddball in life as his enhanced instincts made him.

"Another half hour and we'll be there," J.D. announced over the intercom.

"Good," she muttered. "One more step away from Mr. I'm-in-Charge."

Typical woman, sniping because she didn't like him telling her what to do. He annoyed her? Good. Because she bugged the shit out of him.

The rest of the ride passed in steady, if not comfortable, silence.

The next morning, Alex groaned as the doorbell rang. She glanced at her alarm clock. At least whoever had decided to visit had waited until nine. She walked by her spare bedroom, where Cole had insisted he stay to play bodyguard. She snorted. *As if. He's sleeping like the living dead while I'm getting the door.* In his defense, he had put in a full night bartending to continue his cover.

"Coming," she called when the bell rang again. Through the peephole, she saw her uncle. She opened the door in surprise. When she'd arrived at Buchanan Investigations yesterday, Christine had given her a note to expect her uncle at her house later the next afternoon. Not before coffee.

He hugged her, easing her tension in the familiar warmth of his arms.

"I was worried about you, girl," he said gruffly and walked with her into the living room. He looked around him with a question. "No coffee?"

Alex huffed and made a fresh pot while her uncle waited in the living room. After a few minutes, the coffee perked. Alex poured him a cup and joined him on the couch. "Not that I'm not glad to see you, but what's up, Uncle Max? This doesn't feel like a social visit. I'm not screwing up the case. Everything's fine. So give."

Max sighed. "I'm worried about you, Alex. You and Hunter don't seem to be getting along, which could jeopardize your safety the deeper we dig into this investigation."

Alex stared at her uncle, torn. At this point, she was in too deep to be pulled. Perhaps the time had come to ask Max about her odd connection to Hunter.

"Uncle Max, I have a question for you." She drew a breath and let it out slowly.

"Yes?"

"Hunter and I seem to react to each other in an...odd way."

"Desire isn't odd, Alex. It's a natural response between people who are attracted to one another." The smile in his voice embarrassed her.

"It's not that. I mean, it is. I think he's attractive. But it's more than that. Something strange happens between us, something we can't control."

Max lost his humor fast. "Tell me."

"Well, I've tasted strawberry when I should have tasted coffee. And he tasted coffee when he should have been eating a strawberry pastry."

"What?" Max's soft question stirred the hair on the back of her neck.

"It's like I can experience what he's sensing, and vice versa. But they're flashes of feeling. And I'm not doing it to him on purpose, no matter what he thinks," she muttered. "I'm telekinetic, but that's it. I'm not a telepath or empath, so I don't understand this new ability."

Max watched her. "Has this happened with anyone else?"

"No."

"Damn." His lips twisted and he sighed. "It just figured you'd find someone so—"

"Uncle Max? What are you talking about?"

"Nothing you need to concern yourself with right now. Once this operation is over, I'll explain it all to you. This comes from your father's people, honey. The Saintes have a strange ability that passes through the generations. It appears that it's showing in you. From what I gather, once you and Hunter accept these occurrences, they'll soon stop."

"It's a little off-putting to be doing one thing and feeling something else. The one time I concentrated on not thinking about him, the weirdness vanished. But it seems to come back at odd times, especially when we touch." She coughed to cover her embarrassment.

He gave her a dry look that suggested he did know something of male-female relationships. "Alex, if you feel something for Hunter, my advice is to listen to your heart."

"Didn't you warn me away from him?"

"He's solid, and I'm sure he won't hurt you. You just have to accept that you two have more in common than you might think. If you fight it, Alex, you'll both suffer for it."

"Suffer how?" she asked.

"Just trust me on this. Look, honey, you don't have a typical brain. And I doubt we'll ever understand how your brother's brain works," he murmured. "But I do know that your father and mother experienced the same sensory sharing when they first met."

Alex had a moment's relief before his words registered. She stared at him in horror. "Are you saying I'm going to *marry* Hunter Greye?" She felt lightheaded, and her heart raced.

"No, no," Max hurried to reassure her. "I'm just saying that different people have different reactions to your unique chemistry, that's all. Don't fight it. Just accept it and eventually you and Hunter will ease back into normalcy, or what's normal for us. And, do me a favor, don't tell your brother about this."

"Why not?"

"Because Cole's a lot like me in some ways. He's stubborn, and he likes to think he's always right. Let's let him come to me for the answers, hmm?"

She didn't understand what harm it could do, so she nodded. Besides, this way she wouldn't have to tell Cole anything about her interactions with Hunter. The less said in that direction the better.

Max and she spent the rest of the morning talking about family concerns. Thorne had returned to the small security firm he worked for with Luc and Storm. Her cousins were top-notch problem solvers. Ran in the blood, she thought with a smile. She wondered how long it would take Max to get them working for him. He'd been trying for years.

A little after noon, she kissed Max goodbye and promised to see him at the meeting at five o'clock sharp. She shut and locked the door behind him, then sank back into her couch, wondering about her uncle's bizarre advice.

When he'd mentioned the similarities between her parents' marriage and her situation with Hunter, she'd panicked. She couldn't imagine being in such a volatile relationship with a man. Hunter made her heart thunder and her brain scramble. She remembered her parents being a team, a trusting pair who worked and loved together.

With Hunter, Alex continually found herself in a lesser role to the larger-than-life predator. He intimidated her on a physical level. But it was her overwhelming response to his nearness that bothered her the most. Because she wanted to soothe his aches, to salve his pain and make him feel better. With just a kiss from the hardheaded man, her mind and body became not her own.

Alex didn't want a controlling relationship, and especially

not with a man she barely knew. Granted, the sex would be hotter than hot, but at what price? And wasn't she stepping just a bit outside herself? Hunter hadn't made any pretense about wanting her, but that was about her body. Not as a *girlfriend*, for God's sake. He'd tried to make damn sure she knew her place. Under his thumb and at his beck and call.

She didn't date men she couldn't control. Alex's few boyfriends had treated her like gold, agreeable to anything she wanted. Men she found amusing, fun, refreshing...and men she ultimately left behind.

Hunter was ruthless, powerful, and controlling. He had an honesty and forthrightness about him that J.D. admired. Max said he came from a good family. The man obviously knew his way around the bedroom. She frowned, not wanting to think about where he'd learned his expertise.

But for all his *many* faults, when Alex thought about Hunter, she felt safe, protected, and dammit, cared for. If Max had the right of it, they shared a special bond, one she needed to accept. That didn't mean she had to fall in love with him.

Sudden thoughts of a future with Hunter stirred longings she'd thought long dormant. Alex scoffed at herself. She had a job to do. A job that meant life or death for real people. Acting like a starry-eyed schoolgirl would get her nothing but trouble.

Speaking of trouble... A trip to the spare bedroom showed Cole had made a mess of the covers. He half sprawled on the bed, his big feet hanging over the side in an uncomfortable-looking diagonal spread.

Trust Cole to make even sleeping look hard. Perhaps her uncle had a point about her brother. She loved him dearly, but at times his stubborn arrogance landed him in more trouble than she wanted to handle. He really did take after Max.

Two psychic wonders with alpha tendencies. It was enough

to make a poor girl take stock before diving into the deep end. Her subconscious took note. *So what was Hunter but another psychic wonder with alpha tendencies?* He might as well be family. Horrified at the thought, she left Cole and promised herself that she'd spend the next week gearing up for the auction, her concentration on the mission.

Without Hunter Greye.

Chapter Nine

"You want us to *what?*" Hunter asked with astonishment as he stared at Jurek.

"Just for the next few days. You and Alex need to take what little time you have to grow more comfortable with one another," Jurek repeated patiently. "You need to trust each other. This is Wraith we're talking about introducing you to, a man the Feds haven't managed to arrest after a decade's worth of crime."

More comfortable with one another? Hell. Hunter didn't like the direction this meeting was taking.

"I was thinking she and I could use a break away from all this." *Away from each other.*

"Yeah," Alex agreed wholeheartedly.

Why her agreement irritated him so much he didn't know. A glance around the room showed Cole in agreement, while J.D. and Max took Jurek's side. Thorne, apparently, had finished his part in the investigation, because he hadn't shown for this meeting.

Max shook his head. "When Omaney calls you with details, you won't have much time to move. Alex will have to be with you. So, whether you like it or not, you two need to know how each other thinks and works. It's crucial to this mission and to your safety that you feel a degree of comfort and trust with one another."

"They can do that without living on top of each other all week," Cole protested.

After a moment, Alex sighed. "I'm okay with it. How about you, Hunter?" she challenged, her eyes sparkling.

God, he wanted her. Though it galled him to admit it, even to himself, he was falling for her. The whole package. The stubborn beauty, the sexual temptress, the telepathic wonder. *Shit.*

"No problem on my end." He shrugged. He'd be damned if he'd look like the weak link here.

"Good, then it's all settled. I'll arrange for you two—" Jurek began, only to have Hunter interrupt him.

"We'll stay at my place. I've got the facilities to accommodate us both and keep track of what's going on with Westlake. No one but you knows where it is, so we'll be perfectly safe."

"You'd better be," Max added, his voice gruff. "That's my niece you're taking with you."

"And my sister," Cole said.

J.D. grinned but had the sense to remain quiet. The little pissant.

Alex frowned. "Maybe I'll be looking after him. Did anybody think of that? Just because he's bigger doesn't mean he's badder."

"The guy can bench press you, Alex. So give the women-power, rah-rah speech a rest," Cole muttered. "Just make sure you keep your head down. Anything seems off, you call us."

"I'm not a kid, Cole. I know what I'm doing."

Cole glanced from her to Hunter, his gaze dark. "I hope so, Sis. I really do."

Hunter turned to Jurek. "And you're still looking into

139

Romero, right? I don't buy Omaney or Wraith hiring him. Something about that hit felt off, disconnected from this case."

Jurek frowned. "I know. Rafe's looking into it for me."

"I thought he was on another case."

"He is, but he told me he'd see to it personally."

Hunter felt better, knowing Rafe had his back. "Good." He glanced at Alex, wondering how the hell they'd make this work. *I'm a professional. I can do this.* His gaze unerringly fell to her lips, and his most recent fantasies filled his mind's eye. *Shit.*

The room fell into an awkward silence, and Hunter hoped like hell Max wasn't reading his thoughts.

Jurek said slowly, "Well then, no time like the present. Alex, Hunter, good luck to you both. I'll be in touch throughout the week. But the biggest thing you two can do to help is develop some trust. Remember, Rebecca's depending upon you."

They stood and nodded. Alex looked like Hunter felt—grim but resigned.

Cole looked as if he wanted to belabor the point, but Max gripped him by the arm. They stared at one another for a moment, but neither said anything.

"I'll see you in a week." Alex hugged her brother and uncle. "Don't worry. I'll be fine. Just make sure you're ready to go in once we find out where he's keeping them."

Hunter waited for her. They left the building together in a quiet procession.

"You brought your car, right?" Hunter asked to break the silence.

"Yes."

"I've got your address. Why don't you take some time to pack while I take care of a few things at home? I'll pick you up

140

around seven tonight, okay?"

Alex nodded and he left, mentally listing what he'd need to be ready for her arrival.

At seven o'clock, he rang her doorbell. She answered him promptly, and he entered, expecting her to be ready. He sighed when he saw that no suitcase sat by the front door.

"I'll just be a minute more. If you're thirsty, there's soda in the fridge." Alex disappeared into her bedroom before he could say a thing.

He helped himself to a drink and moved back into the living room. He and Alex had been ordered to get to know one another better. Fine. He studied the area around him, looking for more details into her personality. The last time he'd been here he hadn't noticed much past Alex's obsession with cleanliness and her body covered in bubbles.

The place was still just as clean as it had been. She didn't have much clutter, and in that they had a good bit in common. She liked comfort, but not opulence. To his surprise, he realized she would probably like his place, since their tastes seemed compatible.

"I'm ready," she breathed as she returned to the living room with a large duffel bag. Without asking, he plucked the large bag from her hands and headed for the door.

"Let's go," Hunter grumbled. "I just hope we don't kill each other before it's all over." *And that I can keep my hands, and my dick, under control. Because just being near you makes me hard.*

Forty-five minutes later they passed yet another farm and turned down a dirt road in the middle of nowhere. Hunter cast a side-glance at his passenger, but could see nothing except curiosity in her study of the woods around them. He drove down the road until he came to his property.

141

A decent-sized farmhouse that he'd completely gutted and refurnished sat next to a three-car garage that he used to house his exercise equipment and vehicle.

The woods surrounded his house, providing a lush wall of protection from prying eyes, though his nearest neighbor lived some five miles away. Just behind the house sat a small lake. He'd purposely built the place on it. On his few days off, Hunter spent his mornings staring out over the water, watching as the sun rose like a warm watercolor over his land.

"It's nice," Alex said, looking surprised.

"You thought I lived in a shack in the woods, maybe?" he asked and saw her blush.

"Very funny." She grabbed for her bag. Again, Hunter plucked it out of her hands and ushered them both toward his front door. He entered a series of codes before it opened and waited for Alex to precede him.

The moment she stepped over the threshold, he realized how much he wanted her to like it here. She was the first woman to see the place since he'd built it after his breakup with Anna. Even his mother had yet to visit, simply because he was rarely home.

Simple and plain, his walls and furniture held none of the brightness of Alex's home, yet retained the same sense of comfort. It had a rustic look—cream-colored walls, wooden beams for support, and hardwood flooring covered the front rooms.

Paintings of battles lined his walls, his only foray into art collecting. He watched Alex examine his house, moving around to note the fine film of dust coating the neat stacks of newspapers and clear tabletops. Crap, he knew he'd forgotten something. She tested out the soft leather chair and sofa with thoughtful consideration.

"Are you through yet?" he asked, amused. When she glanced up at him with a grin, his heart raced. He had a sudden urge to show her his bedroom.

"You know, Hunter, I never would have pegged you as a guy with such a tasteful home."

"Thanks," he said wryly.

"But I have to admit this place is comfortable. Show me the rest." She stood and waited.

Hunter took her through the kitchen—a large, open room with a counter overlooking the living room. They briefly toured his study and then ventured down the hall to the bedrooms.

"You have a choice," he rumbled, thoughts of beds and Alex making him twitchy. "You can sleep in either of these spare rooms." He motioned to twin rooms connected by a bathroom.

The rooms, like the rest of the house, were done in neutral tones. Both had carpeting in a thick tan weave. Simple oak dressers and closets were all that stood in the rooms beside the full-size beds.

"Not too creative in there, eh?" Alex teased.

He shrugged. "My room's down the hall." When they walked back out into the hallway, Alex looked toward his room but made no move to approach. Hunter could feel the subtle change in her and knew she felt as he did, uncomfortable with her body's wants.

"Okay." She turned to face him. "I'll take this one." Nodding, he grabbed her bag and dropped it in with her.

Their solitude suddenly smothered him, and he felt an urgent need to escape, to tamp down his desires.

"I'll let you get settled in while I catch up on a few things in the study. Yell if you need me." He left before he could give in to the impulse to touch her once more, curious to see if the silken remembrance of her skin had been all in his mind. And knowing it hadn't been.

Alex sighed as she watched him go. Max had told her to accept her feelings for Hunter and not to fight their connection so hard. But Alex didn't yet know how she felt about the enigmatic man who made her pulse rocket.

She wondered if she ought to just confront Hunter about their obvious unease with one another. Surely two professionals could agree to work together and ignore the heated chemistry between them.

As Alex unpacked, she considered the best way to approach Hunter about the matter. But the sight of a blooming geranium on her nightstand stopped her.

She stared at the flower, her gaze drawn to the vibrant red petals. She peeked into the other guest room and saw a pink geranium sitting in a similar position on the nightstand. Then she remembered the many plants throughout his house. It was oddly telling of his character that he had surrounded himself with life.

Hunter didn't seem a man of many words. The innate stillness in his being seemed to suggest a thoughtfulness, an enduring patience that she'd found curiously absent in his dealings with her. For a solitary man, his devotion to the living things in his home hinted at a need for companionship.

Then again, maybe she was reading more into this than there was. But she couldn't deny that Hunter's collection of plants added another fascinating dimension to the man, as did the tasteful art on the walls. Not a naked girlie calendar in sight, she thought with a smile.

She'd noted a Rocco and a Stiver in the living room, prints by two accomplished artists who depicted the Civil War in all its glory. She'd also noticed a few nature scenes and resolved to look again later.

A yawn and growing lethargy convinced her to nap. Giving in to the urge to relax, Alex curled up in the soft bed and gave way to sleep. It didn't surprise her when her thoughts drifted, once again, to Hunter Greye.

Alex woke to the scent of something incredible. She sat up and pushed a soft blanket from her body, uncomfortable at the thought of Hunter putting it on her and seeing her while she slept. She quickly stood and stretched. Then she ran a brush through her hair and left her room to follow the wonderful aroma coming from the kitchen.

The windows showed the deepening evening. Bright halogen lights illuminated the granite counter upon which he worked.

Busy stirring something that appeared to be spaghetti sauce, Hunter looked very male and yet very much at ease in his kitchen.

"What's for dinner?" Alex shoved her hands in her back pockets and rocked on her heels as she watched him work.

"Spaghetti and my famous sauce," he said without turning to face her.

"Sounds and smells great." Silence filled the room. "Um, can I help?"

Hunter nodded to the refrigerator. "Yeah, you can grab me a beer." Alex handed him one, then grabbed one for herself. She sat at the counter and watched him.

He finished stirring and turned with the counter to his back, nursing his beer while he studied her.

"Thanks for the blanket," Alex blurted.

"You looked cold." He shrugged and continued to stare at her.

She saw more than lust in his gaze. Confusion, interest, and...affection? The possibility staggered her. What if Hunter felt the same longing she did? What if he wanted more from her than a roll between the sheets? What then?

She cleared her throat and told herself to stop daydreaming. "What? What are you staring at?"

"I'm just getting to know you," he said sarcastically, and Alex could see that he didn't appear overjoyed to have her in his home.

So much for the affection she thought she'd seen in his eyes.

"You know, you and Cole look a lot alike, yet very different." Hunter cocked his head in contemplation. "You've both got the same coloring, the same jade green eyes that darken when you're pissed off. Yet he looks like a miniature Max, while you..."

"While I...?" she prodded.

"You don't." He frowned. "You know why we're here, right?"

Alex nodded. *Time to straighten things out, finally.* "Yes. We need to work together on this case, and we need to be able to trust each other implicitly. And quite frankly, right now, we don't."

Hunter nodded but didn't say anything, his eyes hooded as he stared at her.

"I think we're uncomfortable with each other and not just because we work for different firms. This odd link we seem to share isn't helping." Alex decided to tell him what Max had told her. "My uncle told me something today."

"What did he say?"

146

"He said that whatever's happening between us is a Sainte thing. Apparently, you're reacting to my brain chemistry. He said it's no big deal and to just accept it."

Hunter set down his beer and moved around the counter to stand by her. "Accept it? How exactly?"

Alex eyed him warily. Looming over her the way he did, Hunter looked fierce.

"It's not as easy as it sounds, Alex. It's pretty disconcerting to suddenly find yourself feeling things you know come from someone else." His eyes seemed to burn as he studied her. "I know we need to work closely together to solve this case. I can try to do that."

"Good." Alex tried not to look as nervous as she felt. Being this close to Hunter made her nerve endings tingle. She had to fight to keep herself from overtly staring at his firm lips, her memories of their kisses constantly teasing her.

"I'm trying to accept this," Hunter said softly, looking at her with a subtle difference she couldn't put her finger on. He closed his eyes and breathed deeply. When he opened them, he surprised her with a feral grin. "I have to tell you, though, that right now I feel warm, very warm and very hungry." Before she could ask what he meant, he lowered his mouth to capture hers.

Hunter brought her to her feet and pulled her into his embrace while his mouth remained fixed to hers. When he licked past her lips, she sighed, and when he thrust his tongue into her mouth, she moaned.

He pulled back. "How's that for accepting?" Hunter asked huskily before he bent to rob her of speech again.

His large body was both graceful and strong as he caged her in his hold. He stroked her back, creating a heat that pooled in her stomach and worked its way down her limbs and into her womb. When he rocked into her, he thrust in a rhythm that told her where this path they ventured on would lead. And God help her, she didn't want to stop.

Minutes later, Hunter ended their embrace and rasped, "That's about as accepting as I can be with my clothes on."

Alex felt like a limp noodle when he sat her back onto the stool and put the counter between them.

"What..." Alex had to clear her throat. "What exactly was the purpose behind that little display?"

"For one thing, it wasn't so little." Hunter chuckled at her blush.

"*Hunter*," she warned with a look.

"It was just a little test I'd given myself. I wanted to see if I had the discipline to pull away from you. I did," he said, though he didn't sound pleased.

Alex frowned, annoyed that their kisses had been no more than an experiment to him. Did the man have no concept of honest passion? "Yes, well, that's going to have to stop. We need to focus on Wraith and Omaney, not your libido. You're just going to have to work on controlling yourself," she said loftily.

He glared at her and leaned over the island in her direction. "Well, sweetheart, it wasn't *my* lust ruling me just then. As a matter of fact, I was accepting, like you told me to do. I acted on what *you* were feeling."

Alex glared back at him, ignoring the heat in her cheeks. "Cut the crap. That wasn't a huge flashlight in your pocket. We're drawn to each other. So what? It's just chemistry. Bottom line is that we have to trust one another. And right now, I don't trust you very much."

"Join the club," he muttered. "Look, we have a few days to build this partnership." He sighed, obviously not wanting to share any more of himself than he had to. "But we don't have to do it all tonight. How about some dinner, and then we'll break 'til tomorrow?"

"Good idea. What did you have planned?"

He served her a plate of dinner and grabbed his own. "I was thinking we could use tomorrow to study each other's defensive maneuvers. Because when we finally do encounter Wraith, we'll have to fight our way out of the place. And I can't go into a dangerous scenario without knowing what your skills are."

Granted, of the two of them, she was the weaker candidate. But he didn't have to make her so aware of it. She didn't give him the satisfaction of a response and ate her dinner. Afterward, she cleaned up—since he'd cooked—and joined him in the living room. She noticed several plants. Lots of green, but no color. Inspiration struck.

Reaching for a newspaper he'd left on the table, she settled onto the couch. "Hunter?"

"Yeah?" He sat across from her with a book. *The Art of War.* Figured.

"Thanks for the flowers. I like them." He flushed and tried to shrug her off as if he hadn't heard her. "*Very* thoughtful," she added and stifled a laugh at his frown. So, the man with trust issues had a softer side. *She knew it.* Her good mood restored, she read the news before turning in for the night.

The next morning, Hunter sat calmly on his porch and watched the sunrise. Beautiful, he thought as he watched the fading indigo brighten through a blanket of clouds into the pale blue sky before him.

He felt Alex approach before he saw her. Closing his eyes, he inhaled her flowery shampoo and grew hard at the thought of her naked in the shower. Why the hell did she, of all people, have the power to make him want so badly?

"Beautiful," she murmured, echoing his earlier sentiments.

"This is my favorite part of being home," he admitted. He felt her studying him, but said nothing more.

She left, only to return moments later. "Uh, Hunter? You don't have any coffee, do you?"

"It's in the cupboard next to the stove. I keep it just in case of company." He didn't want to disclose that he'd bought it yesterday for her. Or that he'd bought the flowers, thinking that she might like them.

"Yes," she sighed and left him, presumably to fuel her caffeine addiction.

Hunter stared out at the sky and thought long and hard about the decisions he'd reached last night.

He and Alex had more than a mere mental connection. Her uncle had said that they should simply accept it. But Hunter didn't think he could do that without making love to her. He'd surprised himself last night with his restraint. Just tasting Alex's ripe lips made him want to forget everything but fucking her. Maybe if they finally broke down and had sex, this constant yearning would disappear.

Hunter never lost control with anyone. Even when he'd been engaged to Anna, he'd wanted her, but he'd been able to control himself. With Alex, he'd come in his damned *pants*. His common sense deserted him at a whiff of her scent.

He shook his head as he pondered the problem. The more he thought about it, the more he realized that he and Alex should get this issue out in the open and deal with it here, in the safety of his own home.

Minutes later, Alex returned. "This is wonderful," she said as she sipped her coffee.

"After breakfast, I'd like to start in the barn. I've got some mats in there that we can use. I want to see what you can do."

"Fine. But not until I've finished my coffee."

Hunter left her sitting on the porch and entered the garage. There, he engaged in some stretching and early-morning exercises. When Alex joined him, he had worked up a light sweat and felt limber enough for their workout.

She wore shorts and a T-shirt. He only wore shorts. Perfect for maximum flesh-to-flesh contact.

After Alex finished stretching—*good Lord the woman had legs*—she approached him. She blinked at his chest and did her best to look away, yet her gaze strayed back to him time and time again.

"Okay," he said gruffly. "I'm going to come at you, and I don't want you to pull any punches. Treat me like your average mugger. Gimme some of those moves you used in Omaney's warehouse."

"Warehouse? I don't know what you're talking about," she protested with a grin on her face.

"Stubborn woman."

She positioned herself at the ready, knees bent, arms loose, her fists chest-high and ready to move. He tested her reflexes, not surprised when she countered his every attack. She had well-timed and well-placed kicks that kept him distanced enough not to do any real damage.

Then he changed tactics and tried to sweep her off her feet. She danced around him, landing some hard punches to his midsection. He remained unhurt, but a lesser-built man might feel some pain.

"Not bad," he said and circled her, pleased when she moved with him.

He feinted left, then tackled her with a brute strength he'd been holding back. Her breath whooshed from her body as she slammed against the mat. Worried that he'd used more strength than he should have, Hunter eased up, only to have her thrust him away and nearly geld him in the process.

"You cheated," he said with annoyance when he stood to face her.

"No, you underestimated me." She grinned and jumped back out of his reach.

Hunter wouldn't make that mistake again. He tuned in to his inner awareness, seeing the vulnerabilities he hadn't seen before.

"Hunter?" Alex asked cautiously. She sensed something different come over him. He knew because he'd intentionally projected it. Apparently, their connection went both ways.

"Accept it, Alex. Remember what your uncle said, hmm?"

"Maybe we should take a break." She narrowly avoided his lunge.

Hunter laughed in a low purr and continued to stalk her. He was having fun for the first time in a long time. "Come on, Alex. Show me what you've got. So far, I'm impressed."

"I think we're at an impasse. Let's try something else."

But Hunter already had something else in mind. He launched himself at her and flattened her on her back, pinning her to the mat beneath him.

She gasped. "You're fast." Squirming, she brushed against him in ways he could no longer ignore. "Hunter, move."

He stared down at her and knew the time had come. "No, Alex." He nipped at her throat. "I think it's finally time we stopped dancing around the truth."

Chapter Ten

"What?" Alex asked nervously but didn't break his stare.

"I need you, Alex. And you need me. I feel it every time you look at me." He groaned and kissed her. "Yes," he murmured and leaned toward her lips. "I definitely think it's time."

She opened her mouth hungrily under his, and he took her acceptance gladly. His blood pumped and desire raced through his body, filling him with the urge to finally claim her.

"That's it, angel," he said softly before plunging his tongue into her mouth. He kissed her with all the pent-up passion he'd been feeling since he'd met her. And he almost exploded when she returned it wholeheartedly.

Needing to feel her naked body against his own, he quickly drew them both to their feet, then proceeded to strip her out of her clothing.

"Shit, you are so damned beautiful. You make me ache." He felt shaky and confused at the intensity of emotion accompanying his lust. He wanted to make this right for her more than he wanted completion for himself. Watching her eyes darken to that emerald green turned him on more than he'd thought possible.

He hurriedly stripped and they stared at one another with awe.

"Hunter." Alex sighed. "You're so strong," she marveled and touched his chest with a soft hand.

He closed his eyes as she stroked his chest, arms, and abdomen. As her hands moved lower, it was all he could do not to throw her down and thrust into her greedily. When her hands closed over the hard length of him, he thrust against her palms, needing to shove her thighs wide and plunge deep. She slid her thumb over the top of him, spreading the evidence of his desire.

"*Fuck*, Alex," he moaned.

"You're wet for me. So hot and hard," she murmured as she stroked him.

Hunter couldn't take any more. He lowered her to the ground and covered her, ecstatic at the feel of her curves under him. "Alex, angel, please. I need you." Thoughts of condoms faded as instinct consumed him. He could think of nothing more than his hunger to forge strong ties to this woman.

He kissed her ravenously, aching where they touched. His moved his lips over her mouth and neck to suckle at her ripe breasts. She mewed with desire, moaning his name, and he trembled with the effort to make it last.

Alex cried out as his lips left her breast, only to return to the other. She felt as if she were burning, needing Hunter as much as she needed breath. The things he did to her body... She arched into his mouth as his teeth closed over her nipple. "*Hunter.*" She thrust her hands into his silken hair, holding him to her.

She had never felt anything so right in her life.

"God, yes," he purred as he kissed his way down her belly.

She writhed beneath him, wanting to end the blaze

consuming her. She felt so empty, so needful. And only Hunter could fill her. When his lips found her clit, she spread her legs wider. Alex couldn't stop the tremors shaking her, nor could she stop the flow of emotion surging through her body.

"Hunter, please," she pleaded. "I want you inside me."

He sucked hard and she cried out, so close to ecstasy. Then he blanketed her with his body. She could feel him poised to enter, his thick shaft at her entrance. But he did nothing until she met his fiery gaze.

"Watch me," he ordered huskily and entered her slowly, stretching and filling her with his vitality. The pained hunger on his face shook her, and as they slowly became one, she knew she would never be the same again.

His breathing grew labored and Alex urged him for more. "Please," she said and gasped as he thrust his entire length deep. Stuffed full, she could only clench him tight, not wanting their coupling to end.

He groaned her name, his muscles straining as he held himself inside her.

"Oh, yes," she moaned and could only feel as he pulled out, then thrust himself deeper. Over and over, he moved within her until she couldn't take any more. Her desire and his mingled in her mind, the feel of him and the feel of her surrounding him entangled into one entity, straining for perfection.

He rocked again and the pressure on her sensitive flesh pushed her over the edge. "Hunter," she cried as her body exploded into shards of orgasmic bliss. He plunged into her, yelled her name, and shuddered.

The ecstasy pulsed, a roar of pleasure that muted everything but Hunter in her mind.

After a few moments, Hunter leaned up on his elbows and stared down at her. Alex saw a look she'd never before seen on his face. He looked relaxed and, dare she say it, *happy.*

"That was incredible." He lowered his forehead to hers and groaned. "I think you may have killed me."

Alex laughed, sheer joy coursing through her. She felt no remorse or embarrassment for what she'd done. She'd been fighting her feelings for this man for some time now. And she was finally tired of denying herself. Now she only had to figure out what all this meant.

She pulled Hunter's mouth back to hers and kissed him deeply. When he didn't pull away and thickened inside her once more, she jolted. She didn't know how, but her body began tingling all over again.

"Angel, I've been waiting for this forever," he growled, his gaze burning with need. "It's going to take more than just once to relieve all this tension." He began the familiar rhythm, his thrusts overtaking her senses yet again.

"Well then." Alex sighed into his mouth. "Let's relax each other."

When Alex next awoke, she found herself alone in Hunter's bed, a shower running and smooth jazz floating through the room the only sounds in the house.

She stretched and felt a small twinge between her thighs. It had been a very long time since she'd been intimate with a man, and it had never in her life felt as earth-shattering as it had with Hunter.

They had spent all morning learning one another's bodies. And what a thrill that had been. The man touched her in ways she'd never dreamed. With a subtle kiss or caress, he had her body humming like a well-tuned instrument.

She moved and grimaced at the wetness between her legs.

She and Hunter hadn't used protection. The first time, so wrapped up in the overwhelming feelings he'd invoked, she'd been completely oblivious to the thought of birth control. But, after that first time, they'd agreed it wouldn't feel right with anything between them save skin.

Alex was on the Pill and maintained a clean bill of health. Hunter admitted it had been some time for him as well, and she couldn't see him lying about it. The man could be stubborn, autocratic, and at times, bullying. But he'd never put her at risk, especially when he'd done his best *not* to have sex with her from the moment they'd met.

"Alex," he shouted from the bathroom. She walked into the bathroom and stared at his powerful body through the bubbled glass of the shower doors. So strong, yet he'd been so tender with her. She'd never before been with a man who could satisfy her *every time*. He was becoming addicting.

He opened the door and yanked her in with him.

"Hey!"

"Hey yourself," he grumbled. She gasped under the warm water streaming over her. "I thought you were coming in here with me."

"I don't want to be too clingy," she teased and saw his answering smile.

"No, no, angel. Be as clingy as you want." He grabbed the soap, lathered his hands, and ran them over her body. He didn't so much clean her as stoke her into a new frenzy of desire.

Alex could only stare at the primal male before her, entranced by the muscles gleaming under the water, and by the intensity in his eyes as he watched her. Since their first time, he seemed perpetually hard around her.

"Doesn't that ever go down?" She reached out and took him in her hands, stroking with a firmness he liked.

Marie Harte

"Damn," he said on a breath and leaned back against the shower wall. "It's you, Alex. Around you, I can't help myself. What are you doing to me?"

"I wonder if you taste half as good as you look," she asked him thoughtfully.

"Dear God, you do read minds."

She laughed but noted the intense study he gave her mouth.

With a sly smile, she slowly lowered to her knees.

He blocked the raining water with his broad back and widened his stance. The gasp he gave when she took his long, thick cock in her hands satisfied the hungry woman inside her.

"Baby, yeah, do it. Suck me, Alex. Shit." He closed his eyes when she pumped him with her hands.

"Watch."

"Fuck."

She watched his eyelids shutter his expression as she wrapped her lips around the head of his shaft. He palmed the back of her head but didn't pull her closer. He tasted clean, a mixture of raw male, water and a hint of soap. She loved the power in him, but more, she loved how much power she wielded over him like this.

"God, you're so good," he moaned when she cupped his balls in her hand. She stroked his sac and inner thighs while she licked his shaft from base to tip, alternating suction with her strong tongue.

His balls grew tight, and the salty taste of his precome and the trembling of his thighs caused her to grin around him.

"You little witch." He moaned. "Dammit, Alex. I'm trying to hold on, but you're killing me. I'm going to come, baby. So hard. Swallow me."

158

She sucked harder, taking as much of his length in her mouth as she could manage. She didn't think she'd taken much, but he didn't seem to care.

"Yes, yes, baby. *Now.*" He cried out and she sucked him harder, swallowing the jets of seed that filled her mouth.

She'd brought him such pleasure, and the giving made all the difference. He was sighing her name, caressing her head with loving hands.

When she finally finished, she kissed his cock one last time and rose on shaky feet. Tasting him turned her on like nothing else.

"How was that—?"

Before she could finish, he kissed her breathless. And then he went down on his knees.

"Just returning the favor, angel." His smile was the most beautiful thing she'd ever seen.

They didn't leave the shower for a good long time, lost in the magic of each other.

Once clean, dry, and dressed again, Alex left Hunter's bedroom and dropped onto his couch, feeling boneless. She needed a moment to gather her thoughts.

Hunter had a playful side to him that surprised her. In turns, he'd been gentle and giving, rough and demanding. But he'd touched her with something more than carnal devotion. The look in his eyes as he took her spoke more than words could say. The man cared for her. She didn't know how much, but that he did changed everything between them.

Alex had no intention of asking about his feelings or their future together. She wasn't naïve, and she didn't want to ruin things between them when they'd only just started. But she knew this operation was only the beginning. She could only hope the stubborn man wouldn't balk at a future relationship. With Hunter, who knew?

"So, what do you think we should do for an encore?" he asked in a deep voice as he joined her. He bent down for a kiss, and Alex returned it with affection.

"I need a break," she admitted.

He laughed, pleasing Alex at the ease with which his lips now formed a smile. "Me too. Contrary to popular belief, I'm not Superman."

"You could have fooled me."

"You should talk. Around you I'm a walking hard-on."

She blushed. "Hunter."

"Sorry, angel, but that's the truth. Mind you, I'm not complaining." His stomach rumbled. "But you know, I think my stomach is. We need food."

"Good idea."

As they worked together to make sandwiches, Alex took the opportunity to learn more about her lover. *Hunter Greye is my lover. Holy crap.*

They sat down to eat, but Hunter didn't touch his food. "What?" he asked.

"Huh?"

"Why are you looking at me like that?" His eyes narrowed.

"Like what? How am I looking at you?"

"Like you're not sure how to talk to me. I thought we'd *communicated* pretty well today. So, what's wrong?"

"Nothing. I want to know more about you, but I didn't know how to ask," she said bluntly. Hunter, she was coming to learn, was not a man to finesse.

He relaxed. "Hell, Alex. I'm an open book."

She snorted.

"What do you want to know?" He took a huge bite of his sandwich.

"Where do I start? How about telling me how you joined Westlake? J.D. mentioned you'd been in the military."

"J.D. talks a lot," he grumbled. "It's not a secret. My father was a career Marine, and I guess that dedication bled through to my brother and me. I joined the Corps right after college. My, ah, abilities made me a prime candidate for the work I did."

Alex wondered at his hesitation. "Did anyone in the Marine Corps know about your gift?"

"It's not a gift. It just is. And no, because I didn't want them to know. Growing up, we—I—was taught to keep what I could do under wraps. At the time, ugly rumors kept surfacing about a government organization that was investigating psychic phenomena. The people they took for study were never seen again."

Alex nodded. Her uncle had heard the same, rumors about an institute dedicated to exploiting psychic abilities at the expense of their test subjects. Just another reason Uncle Max loathed the government.

"I kept quiet and did my job, but my successes brought me attention anyway. The CIA recruited me, and I spent a lot of time in South America." He frowned.

"What happened?" she asked softly.

"I got engaged. Talk about a mistake. My work took me away from home more and more. Things with Anna didn't work out." He cleared his throat. "Then, one day Jurek showed up at a debriefing. And three months later I was working for Westlake Enterprises."

Alex's mind raced. A fiancée? Dangerous, top-secret missions? *A fiancée?* She had to ask. "Did Anna know about you?"

He grimaced and set down his food. "You mean about my freaky abilities? I told her." He shrugged, as if it were no big deal, but Alex sensed anger, frustration, and pain beneath the casual gesture. "It didn't work out between us, and she left."

"Her loss."

Hunter blinked at her. His lips slowly quirked. "Yeah, her loss." He picked up his sandwich again. "So, what about you?"

"Me? Well, my parents died when I was eleven. Uncle Max, my mother's brother, took us in. He raised us, and we work for him. Not nearly as exciting as your story."

"Oh? I can't move things with my mind."

She flushed. "My entire family is different. My mother and father were both psychic. My uncles are as well."

"Uncles?"

"Max and Uncle Tommy, Thorne and Luc's dad. All of us find our unique talents when puberty hits. It's not pretty." She grimaced. "It takes a while before you can control it. I can't tell you how many boyfriends I lost because I was known as the school freak."

He gave her a commiserating nod. "Which is why I never told anyone what I could do."

"I learned that the hard way. I pretty much keep to myself and do my job. I'm happy."

"Are you?" Hunter asked, his gaze intense.

"I guess. I love my family. It's hard sometimes," she said quietly. "I don't date a lot. I'm a stickler for honesty, and I always feel like I'm being less than honest because I can't share that part of myself."

"Yeah." He took a long swallow of his drink. "I know the feeling."

They sat in silence, staring at one another.

Hunter cleared his throat and stood, breaking eye contact. "So how do you like being a private investigator?"

Alex felt a moment's discomfort. How the hell had the topic veered into her personal problems? "I like it, now that I'm finally allowed to do some field work."

"About that... I don't like you so close to Omaney. I was this close to ripping his guts out when he mauled you in the hotel room the other night."

"I had it under control."

"Did you? Alex, Omaney's not right. He fucking *drugged* you. And he's way too into you for my peace of mind."

"Mine too," she admitted. "I'm not ignorant of the danger, Hunter. I can handle this." And if he thought about taking her away from it, he could think again.

"You're going to have to. I can't keep an eye on you and do my job at the same time." He ran a hand through his hair in frustration. "Dammit, Alex, this is a stupid plan. Taking you to Wraith could be your death sentence. We don't know what we'll find there. What if, by some chance, we find Rebecca, but we lose you?"

"And what if we lose you?" she retorted. "Just because you're a man doesn't make you any less vulnerable to a bullet. Wraith and Omaney are slime. They're dangerous. But so are we."

"We? I know what I'm capable of. So far, the only thing you've done is make me lose my damned mind."

Incensed that he thought so little of her, and worse, that he had cause, she drew on her telekinetic ability. Alex rose to her feet and advanced on Hunter in the kitchen. She slammed him up against the cabinets, holding him there by the sheer force of her mind.

"Shit. Not bad." He tried to push past her restraint, and she increased her focus. "Alex, this side of you is really turning me on."

Gratified by his approval, as well as the humor in his tone, she let him go. "You're really strong. It usually doesn't take so much to hold a person back."

"Good to know." He took her in his arms. "Look, I know how much being in on this op means to you. I just, I worry, okay?" He hugged her. "I thought that sex with you would work you out of my system, but it's only getting worse," he muttered.

"Great, I sound like a disease."

He snorted. "I never know what to make of you. Keeps me off balance." He pulled her with him out the door.

"Where are we going?"

"Back to work. We never did get around to seeing just what you're capable of on the mats. And I need to see it. I need to know you can hold your own, so that I can do what I need to when we meet Wraith."

When we *meet Wraith.* The acceptance she'd been craving for so long felt within reach, and she'd be damned if she'd let it go. Taking the lead, Alex tugged Hunter with her.

"Okay, big guy, but don't complain when I show you how a real woman deals with a problem."

Two hours later, Hunter stared at the ceiling in his makeshift gym, winded and glad of it. Alex could more than hold her own. Between the martial arts training her uncle had insisted she have and her mental mumbo jumbo, the woman had put him on his ass several times. He turned his head and stared at her, more enamored now than he'd been before.

Contrary to what she might think, Hunter prized strength in all forms. Anna had been weak-willed. Alex was anything but. Her telekinesis aside, she had the fortitude to stand up to him. Not many did, man or woman.

"So whose idea was it to break into Omaney's warehouse?" he asked on a breath.

Alex turned on her side and ran a hand over his chest. "Mine. I'm the troublemaker in the family. Just ask my uncle."

He chuckled. "I'm not surprised. So what's the deal with your brother, anyway? The other day, he and I had a discussion, and he nearly had a panic attack."

She froze. "He did?"

"Yeah, he did." All his senses told him there was more to Cole's reaction. But to his disappointment, Alex shrugged him off.

"Who knows? My brother has his quirks. Like we all do."

"Yeah, I guess." It was too soon for blatant honesty, apparently. Then again, Hunter had no intention of telling her everything either, like what had really happened with Anna.

"So, what about your brother?" she asked. "Earlier, you said you were taught to keep your abilities a secret. But you said 'we', then corrected yourself. Is your brother like you?"

Shit. Just more evidence that this woman had burrowed her way under his skin. He didn't talk about Adrian to outsiders. *Maybe she's not an outsider, not anymore.*

"Hunter? If you don't want to talk about him, that's okay."

Why? Because that makes it okay for you to hide details about your family? Irrationally angered she might want to keep parts of herself hidden from him, Hunter growled, "My brother is exactly like me. Adrian is still in the Marine Corps, though. He likes what he can do. The little jerk gets off on it."

"And you don't?" She curled her hand around his biceps. Her touch soothed his tension, like beauty comforting the beast, he thought with amusement. "You seem pretty at ease in your own skin."

"I've worked at it. When I told you I know what I'm capable of, I wasn't bragging. The things I've done… I had good reason, but my abilities, if you can call them that, are pretty primitive. I really am a hunter." Totally bizarre his father would insist on naming him that. "The thrill of the chase heats my blood. I can get too focused, until everything fades but capturing my prey." The hunts, that seething, perpetuating need to conquer, to draw first blood…

"Ah, okay. So was I your prey? You seemed pretty intent on capturing me," she teased and, that easily, she pulled him out of an encroaching darkness.

"You are something I'm trying to figure out."

Alex smiled. "Like a puzzle?"

"Like an addiction," he said thickly, his gaze drawn to her lips. An indrawn breath told him she was growing aroused. The sweetness of her scent deepened, spreading out to infuse his entire body.

"Now, wait a minute," she warned as she tried to scramble to her feet.

Hunter let her rise, then stood. He began stalking her, conscious that this challenge entertained him. There was no need for blood, no sense that he had to trap and kill his opponent. Alex made him want to play.

"Better run, angel. Because when I find you, I'm definitely going to take advantage." He ripped off his shirt and tossed it to the ground.

Her gaze trailed over his sweaty chest to the arousal pushing at his shorts. Alex licked her lips, and he groaned.

"Man, who knew you were this easy?" She laughed and darted out the door. Hunter waited a minute, then gave chase.

He had no intention of losing this prize. The only danger, he admitted to himself, was that he didn't think he *ever* wanted to lose her. And that might prove to be a real problem.

·

Chapter Eleven

Peter walked with quiet arrogance through the spacious hallways of Ray's tropical estate. He'd always admired the cool beauty of the large house, the blues and greens intermingled with the warm corals and bright yellows. Ray's estate, for all its size, felt more like a tropical wonderland than a mansion. Just a small bit of property on an uncharted bit of land near Jekyll Island. A rich man's paradise, and totally private.

He reached the patio overlooking the pool, where Mrs. Simms had directed him. There he found Ray and his detestable assistant, Yasef, involved in conversation.

Yasef stopped mid-sentence as Peter approached. The man's dark brown eyes tracked his every step.

"Greetings, Mr. Omaney," he said with disdain. "Ray, if you'll excuse me?"

Ray chuckled and waved him away, but Peter didn't understand what his friend found so amusing. Yasef was no more than a damned savage, a monster who liked to play unspeakable games and found pleasure in instilling great pain.

"Come, Peter, tell me what you've been up to." Ray smiled, and Peter smiled back, sitting in Yasef's vacant chair.

He stared at Ray for a moment, drawn by his friend's light blue eyes and white-blond hair. The spitting image of his father, which had to eat at him every time he looked in a mirror. Taller than Peter, but thinner, Ray reminded him of a starving artist, those haunted eyes and graceful hands needing only a paintbrush and canvas to complete the picture.

"I wanted to tell you about my meeting with Jed Black." *The bastard who is right now fucking the woman I should have had.* "The arms deal he set up went off like clockwork. The police I'd bribed to take him down a peg disappeared."

"Not a surprise. Black has contacts worldwide. Local police would be easy enough to control."

"Yes, but afterward, there was an incident. A man tried to kill Black."

"Oh?" Ray leaned forward.

"Black shot him without hesitation. He's as cold-blooded and thorough as his reputation claims."

"Do you think Black set it up?"

"If he did, he was pretty convincing." Peter paused. "I made some inquiries. He shot and killed Luke Romero, a gun for hire."

"Interesting. I'm liking Jed Black more and more. And you say he has my angel?"

Peter handed Ray a picture of Alex. "That's her. He nearly raped her on the dance floor. But your angel didn't protest a bit." *Much to my disgust.*

"Perhaps she's already corrupted," Ray murmured. He stroked her picture with a calloused finger. Peter felt a moment's disquiet. Ray had gone off into that other world he sometimes disappeared to. In that frame of mind, his moods were difficult to predict.

Suddenly, Ray dropped the photo and grabbed Peter by the collar. He yanked him so close their faces touched. Peter froze at the menace in Ray's wild-eyed stare.

"How could you leave something so precious in that animal's hands?" he seethed. "That woman might be the one I need. If she's harmed at all, if she bears so much as one mark..." He paused, his rage clearly building.

"It was Jed Black, Ray," Peter said quickly. "I tried to hold onto her, but Black interfered. I know how much the girl might mean to you, but I also figured that getting Black involved in your venture was too good to pass up."

"Maybe it's a little too good to be true, a little too convenient," Ray whispered as he uncurled his fingers from Peter's shirt.

Peter waited until Ray had completely let go of him before moving back out of reach. He did so slowly, not wanting to further enrage his best friend. He knew why Ray lost control, and he knew better than to provoke him. He shouldn't have given him the picture yet.

"You were right, as always, Peter." Ray smiled as if his sudden meltdown hadn't occurred. "I do want Black as well as the woman. I know you don't usually associate with my peers, but this time I'd like you to make an exception. I believe you know a few of them. Congressman Ulie will be here, and I know you and he are good friends."

Peter blinked in astonishment. He hadn't realized Ulie had a dark side.

"Several of my friends in the oil business, as well as a few other prominent businessmen, will be in attendance. Men who can help your career. It's amazing to me that years ago none of them would have given me the time of day. A preacher's son, now a multimillionaire." Ray chuckled. "A good piece of ass can make a man do almost anything." Ray glanced again at the photo on the table. He pocketed it before he stood.

Peter stood as well, and they walked together toward the

beach behind the estate.

"So, tell me more about Alexandra." Ray purred her name and threw his arm companionably around Peter's shoulders. Peter described her in loving detail. Thinking about Alex made his heart race. Remembrances of how pliant she'd been under that small dose of Plezure made him wonder what she'd have been like fully entranced. Could she take his mind from Sarah? Would she be the one to break the spell that sexual creature had woven over him?

He managed to contain his lust, or at least, he thought he had. Ray took him, not to the beach, but to a small guesthouse instead.

"Peter, I can't help noticing your arousal. We both know the only way to save yourself from such sin is to immerse yourself in it. Corruption only works on those bent on denying the truth. But we both know what we are, don't we, my friend?"

Peter wanted to deny him, until Ray pushed open a door and exposed Sarah Moreland, naked and drugged out on the bed in the center of the room.

"Sarah?" he whispered, excited to find her here, of all places.

"Go ahead, Peter. Get her out of your system before it's too late." He watched Ray close the door behind him, and thoughts of Alexandra Tyrell fled his mind as he slowly removed his clothing.

Alex and Hunter spent the next few days going over what-ifs, strategies, and conversations with Jurek, who continued to update them with new information. Apparently, Peter Omaney had resurfaced and continued to go about his daily business. He'd called Jed to send his invitation to the auction. With one more phone call, Jed and Alex would receive notice and be on their way.

J.D. had some luck with Omaney's files. A few of them linked to a man named R.G., and he'd spent the better part of his time figuring out who this R.G. might be. Nothing panned out yet, but he was still looking.

Max was pleased to hear that she and Hunter seemed to be getting along better. She hadn't told him exactly *how* they were getting along, but her uncle hadn't been born yesterday. Cole didn't ask, and she didn't say much more than that her time was well spent.

Hunter was becoming a real problem. The gruff bully she'd first met had disappeared. Though he still liked to get his way, he treated her with respect and a genuine caring—pulling her deeper under his spell. She didn't want to fall in love with him, but against her better judgment, she feared she'd started her decline.

He didn't react when she used her telekinesis to pass the butter. He didn't seem to get enough of her roughness when they sparred. He actually encouraged her to defeat him.

She couldn't believe she'd once thought he didn't want a strong woman. The more she showed him that she could take what he dished out, the more he relaxed around her.

He still growled and grew surly upon occasion, but she didn't mind. That was a part of him. Because after he snapped at her, he worked doubly hard to make her happy. And boy, did he make her *happy.*

The man had a sexual stamina she'd gladly put to the test. Never had she been so aroused around anyone. Sometimes it took little more than the touch of his hand and she wanted to take him to the ground and—

"Yo, angel, you coming or what?"

172

She took a deep breath and forced herself to concentrate on their nature walk. Another thing she really liked about Hunter. He spent much of his time outdoors. She had a feeling the hunter inside him felt hemmed in by walls.

"This path looks well worn," she murmured and skirted another tree root.

"It is. I like to walk by the stream. Lots of crawfish in there, as well as a few salamanders under the rocks."

"You really should have a little boy. Then you and he can terrorize little girls. Just think of all the frogs you could stuff in their pockets."

"Hadn't thought about kids." He shot her an odd look. "But I think about making them all the time."

She flushed. "Very funny. I wasn't saying you and I should have one." He stopped in front of her, and his smile faded. *Crap, can I put my foot farther in my mouth?* "I just meant that... Oh, never mind," she huffed and walked around him.

When he didn't follow her, she snapped, "Well, come on. These are your woods, not mine."

Just because she'd been fantasizing about a life with Hunter didn't mean it would ever happen. Sure, she wanted to continue to see him after this operation, but Hunter didn't seem like the family type. Look at how he froze at mention of a child. And what the hell was she babbling about children for anyway? Sure she wanted kids, but not *now*.

Hunter slapped her on the butt. "Testy, aren't we?"

He passed her, and she followed him to the magical stream he'd mentioned while she was forcing herself to calm down.

"This is one of my favorite spots," he admitted and sat on a large boulder. Alex joined him, and they watched the light sparkle off the small river of water running over rocks and patches of moss. Sunlight streamed through the canopy of leaves overhead, turning the woodland site into an ethereal vision of solitude.

The weather had cooled with each day spent at Hunter's house. Instead of unending humidity, a comfortable warmth settled under the breeze that pushed through Alex's hair. Clad in shorts and T-shirts, the pair of them looked like they were on vacation instead of preparing for a potentially lethal job.

"This feels like paradise."

Hunter shifted her off the boulder and into his lap. "Yeah, it does." He kissed the top of her head and held her close.

Dammit. He kept doing things that made her want to hold him and never let go. He brought her coffee each morning, and he added just the right amount of milk and sugar. He liked many of the same books and movies she did, though his taste for action-adventure movies outweighed her preference for romantic comedies. Still, he'd found a few and watched them with her, holding her in his arms the way he did now.

Though Alex knew she and Hunter had been forced to spend their time together, for her, it was anything but a hardship. She dreaded the end of their stay. Sighing, she held his arms tighter to her chest.

"Alex?"

"Hmm. What?"

"You okay?" Hunter turned her in his arms to face him and kissed the base of her throat, stirring her into a desire that, with him, always stayed close to the surface. She couldn't help squirming over his taut lap.

"You're good at that," she rasped and ran her hands over his shoulders. "Too good."

"How can a man be too good when kissing his woman?"

Hunter asked with a grin.

Her heart raced. *His woman?* "I'm nobody's woman." *As much as I want to be.* She was afraid to hope.

"Funny, because you're in *my* arms squirming on top of *my* dick. Want to try that one again?" He squeezed her tighter.

"You like it rough, don't you?" She loved how hard he felt beneath her.

"So do you, angel." He nipped her earlobe before easing his tongue into her ear, a move that never failed to put her into immediate, uncontrollable lust.

She moaned and ground against him. Just what she needed to put her mind back on track. Some mind-blowing sex with Hunter. *Time to shelve my emotional issues.*

She wriggled out of his hold and hopped down from the boulder. When he pushed off and moved to follow, she held him back with her mind. She allowed her gaze to wander down his frame to center on his groin. "Tell you what, sexy. If you can beat me back to the house, I'll concede."

"Concede what?" he asked in a gritty voice.

"Whatever you want."

"Deal," he breathed.

"But if I make it back to the house before you catch me, you're mine for the next twenty-four hours."

"No problem." He didn't sound worried at all.

She frowned. "That means I can make you wait on me hand and foot while you're naked. I can make you paint your toenails and sing on top of a table, and you have to do it."

"Sweetheart, stop. You're giving me all kinds of ideas."

"I get a five-minute head start." They'd spent twenty minutes walking to the stream. She figured five minutes was fair.

"Five or ten, doesn't matter. I'm picturing you waiting on me, hand and foot, while *you're* naked. We should have thought of this before."

"Laugh it up, *sweetheart*. See you at the house."

Alex raced back along the trail. Either way, she couldn't lose. Some light fun, a sexy interlude, and the loss of these maudlin thoughts. What more could she ask for from the man she considered hers...for the next few days?

Running hard, she moved at top speed through the trail. She hadn't heard Hunter at all, and figured she'd had too much of a head start. But she refused to slow down. Imagining Hunter at her beck and call until tomorrow was too good a fantasy to pass up. At the house, she bent over to catch her breath. Once relaxed, she stood up and waited. And waited some more.

"Miss me?" he whispered from behind her.

She jumped, startled from her exhaustion. "When the hell did you get here?"

"A few minutes before you did." The grin on his face had her taking a step back. "Now, angel, what was that about twenty-four hours? You'll concede whatever I want?"

His excitement aroused hers to a fevered pitch. "What do you want?"

"Everything, Alex. Everything."

Moments later, in his bedroom, Hunter stared at Alex, aware of her heady arousal. Fuck, her scent was killing him. "Take off your clothes."

She bit her lip, as if nervous, but he could see her desire. Her shallow breaths, flushed cheeks, and pebbled nipples told him better than words that his angel wanted him. But how much could she take, especially if he let himself really go?

Dreading the thought of her leaving the way Anna had, Hunter reined in his hungers and promised to just enjoy himself. He and Alex only had a few more days. Why not enjoy having a sexy woman at his beck and call for hours? What more could a man want?

Trust, his conscience whispered. *Love. A true partner in every sense of the word.*

Everything.

Angry that he couldn't simply enjoy the moment, he didn't notice Alex's stillness until she cleared her throat.

"Why are you still dressed?" he growled.

"Why are you so mad? You won." Her hands rested at the hem of her shirt.

"What did I win?" he asked, incensed that she seemed perfectly capable of having sex with him, but she didn't trust him enough to share details about her family's abilities.

Alex dropped her hands to her sides. "I don't understand you. We were having fun, a race to the end. You won, I lost, and we were just about to have some incredibly hot sex. What put your panties in a bunch?"

Her tart response pushed him past rational. He yanked her to him and kissed her hard, willing at least one of them to understand what he felt, because he had no idea about what he needed.

She resisted him for a moment, and then she sighed into his embrace and hugged him closer.

"Hunter," she breathed when he left her mouth to trail kisses down her neck. "Don't be mad, baby. Let me make you feel better."

She removed his clothes in between kisses. Then she took

off her shirt and shorts, leaving herself in a sexy bra and panties that he wanted to rip off with his teeth. The survival instinct that had pulled him out of more shit than he wanted to remember told him to claim this woman. Not any woman, not Anna, or the string of meaningless conquests he'd had since her meant a tenth of what Alexandra Sainte did. And it scared him to death.

More than just sex, being with Alex was a balm to his soul. She understood him on so many levels. Despite their differences, they had much in common. Too much to blow off by reducing their relationship to nothing but mutual desire.

As Alex kissed her way down his body, from his mouth and chin to his chest, he watched her like the predator he was. "You're mine," he rasped.

He didn't know what to expect, but the longing in her gaze took him aback. She shuttered the look so fast he might have imagined it, but the softness of her kisses, the sure, soothing pressure of her touch, told him he'd witnessed the truth. Perhaps Alex wasn't as immune to the growing affection between them as he'd thought.

His breathing grew erratic as her hands stroked his belly and lower, following with her mouth. He wanted to conquer her, to tame her, but she held the power now, and she knew it. He loved her strength, her power. And he wondered again if she would bolt or accept him if he decided to show her the truth about himself.

"Alex," he hissed as she took him in her mouth. She loved him so generously, so completely, that he found himself close to climax all too soon. *Too soon to feel this way, to feel this love...*

Hunter fisted his hands in her hair and tugged her away from him. "Get naked and get on the bed," he ordered.

She did so quickly, her desire clear.

"Lie back and spread your legs."

"Hunter," she moaned but did as ordered.

"You're mine, Alex. The way you respond doesn't lie." He didn't give her a chance to argue. Hunter put his mouth over her clit and gave her the pleasure she gave him by simply being. At turns gentle, then rough, he surrendered to the desire obliterating everything but the need for Alex.

A part of him regretted her birth control that prevented conception. When she'd mentioned a child earlier, an unfamiliar yearning struck him mute. He could too easily imagine Alex round with his child. A small boy with her eyes and his abilities, a young girl with her mother's beguiling looks and strength of will.

"Mine," he rasped before he rose from his position between her legs and covered her. He nudged her thighs wider and thrust deep, enraptured by the ecstasy on Alex's face. The pleasure of her expression prodded him to give her more, to see her explode with the passion they created together.

Heat built as he deliberately ground against her pelvis, rocking against that taut nub that signaled her arousal.

"Hunter," she cried out. "Yes, yes."

Alex tightened around him and clung, groaning her pleasure. But it wasn't enough.

"Give it to me, Alex." He sent a surge of desire through their special connection, telling her without words what he needed.

She shook her head, still shivering in her climax.

Pressure built at the base of his spine. His balls drew tight, his cock swelled, and he knew his orgasm was a breath away.

"I need to hear it." *Say it, Alex. Say you love me.* He tried, but he couldn't wait.

She cried out when he surged deeper and came inside her.

He couldn't stop the ecstasy crashing over him in a wave so intense he saw stars. He surged and spent, and still he moved within her. The primitive power he possessed came to the surface, drawn to the angel in his arms. Despite his intention to keep it down, it—*he*—demanded Alex's surrender. He wouldn't take anything less.

Their orgasms didn't matter. Hunter wasn't sure how he actually did it, but that foreign part of him moved deeper into Alex's mind and seized control. Absolute power she couldn't escape from unless he allowed it. And he was helpless to stop himself.

With strong, deep strokes, he pushed them both toward a completion neither was ready for. It should have been impossible for Hunter to continue. Alex, he could sense, needed more time to recover. Yet their hungers rose. Sensation flowed between them, back and forth, his then hers, until they were no longer separate people, but one heart, one mind, crying out their perfect bliss.

Moments later, Hunter came back to himself. Panting, he rested on his hands over Alex, their bodies still joined. The painful need to release no longer drove him, and he withdrew from her warmth, scared of how she'd react. He moved next to her, anxious and angry with himself. He hadn't meant to go so far, but Alex got to him on a level even Anna had never reached.

If he'd scared her away, he'd never forgive himself. He—

"I'm a mess," Alex panted. "Did I imagine that? *Oh my God.* Hunter, you nearly killed me. You're a sexual maniac."

He tensed, disgusted at his own lack of control.

Gradually, Alex's breathing deepened, and she snuggled into the pillow beneath her head. "*My* maniac." She drifted off to sleep with a smile on her face.

Hunter stared at her, unable to believe what he'd heard.

Unable to stop himself from hoping. He settled next to her and watched as she slept.

Chapter Twelve

When Alex woke, she heard Hunter outside the room speaking in a low voice. She left the bed, threw on Hunter's shirt, and exited the bedroom for the living room. Hunter stood by the kitchen counter, wearing nothing but a pair of jeans. *You sexy, sexy man.*

She saw a cell phone in his hand. "Jurek, I got the call. A small jet will be waiting for us in Brunswick, not Savannah International." Hunter paused and nodded. "Yeah, that would be too easy. What? Okay. Send me what you have on the players and I'll get on it." He paused again, a frown settling over his face. "Alex is fine. She's sleeping right now. Why? Because it's almost midnight, Jurek! She's fine. Really. We're good for tomorrow. Yeah, I'll call you then." Hunter closed his cell phone.

Alex ran her fingers through her hair, still feeling slightly dizzy. She still wasn't sure exactly what had happened with Hunter, but whatever it was, she wanted to do it all over again, provided she could still walk.

Hunter placed his cell phone on the counter and turned around. He froze when he saw her.

"What? No 'Thank you, ma'am'?" she teased.

He flushed and shook himself out of the tension gripping him. "Hell, Alex. That was a helluva lot more than *wham bam.*" Crossing to her, he took her in his arms.

"You're telling me." She sighed and relaxed into his hug. "When can we do it again?"

He barked a laugh and swung her around off her feet. "You always keep me guessing. Just when I think you'll say or do one thing, you do another."

Confused, Alex smacked him to put her down. "What? I should have yelled at you for giving me an orgasm?"

His mirth died, and she didn't like the somberness that closed his features. "It was more than a simple orgasm, Alex, and you know it."

"We're not simple people, Hunter. I had a great time, you had a great time, I guess I'm just not seeing the problem."

He sighed and walked away from her. Slumping into a stuffed leather chair, he regarded her from under hooded eyes.

After several moments of silence, Alex wanted to burst. "Okay! I give up. I hate you. You're an ogre. And you're way too bossy. Happy now?"

He shook his head. "It doesn't bother you that I took you so hard? That I made you...that I controlled the sex?"

"No."

He seemed baffled. "No? That's it?"

"What else is there to say? You made my bones melt. Are you looking for compliments?" She knew he wasn't, but she had no idea what bothered him.

"So you didn't mind when I took control of you like a puppet? I forced you to orgasm."

"Promise to do it again, and we'll call it even." She grinned, but the horrified look on his face told her she'd said the wrong thing. "Hunter, what the hell is wrong with you?"

"I don't understand."

"Neither do I." Sudden comprehension flashed through her,

though she couldn't have said what sparked it. Perhaps she and Hunter were still connected in that special way. "This has to do with the ex, right?"

He closed his eyes and leaned his head back. Without looking at her, he spoke very quietly. "Anna and I were happy for a time. My work took me farther and farther away. I thought that was why we'd begun to drift apart. But my mother told me I was a fool to want to marry a woman I couldn't be totally honest with. Shows you what she knows," he said, as if to himself.

Alex leaned closer, enthralled by this look into Hunter's past.

"I came home for a thirty-day leave, the longest I'd ever taken. I spent all of it with Anna. We grew close again, closer than I'd ever been with another woman."

"How long ago did all this happen?" Alex asked softly.

"A few years ago, before I signed on with Jurek." He swallowed loudly. "I'd thought about what my mother said. And she was right, really. How could I be honest with my feelings for Anna if I wasn't honest about everything? I mean, she fell in love with me, but she didn't know the real me."

Alex understood what he said, probably more than he imagined.

"When I told her, she didn't believe me. So I showed her. It freaked her out at first, but she tried to come around. I was so happy she'd accepted me, I let myself go. I..." He paused and opened his eyes, searching hers for something. Understanding, acceptance, she didn't know.

"You what, Hunter?"

"I showed her. I let down the barriers between us. When she and I made love, the hunter inside me, the most primitive part of me, took control."

Realization dawned. "You took charge of her body and pushed her past her limits, right? Like you did with me." Alex didn't know how to feel. Jealous that he'd once shared this with Anna, and ecstatic that he had just shared all of himself with her.

He nodded, his face grave. "With her, I meant to. But, Alex, with you, it just happened."

"So you're waiting for me to freak out on you and leave, like she did."

"No. I know you won't leave. We have a job to do."

She wanted to smack him for sounding so cold, but the bleakness in his eyes stole her resolve. "Men really are idiots."

He blinked. "What?"

"Did it never occur to you to just tell me how you felt without me having to drag it out of you?"

He stiffened. "I just told you what happened. I never said anything about feelings."

You're mine. How many times had he said that to her before proving it most emphatically? Used to stubborn men, Alex knew better than to force him to talk. By the time she finished with him, he'd be begging her to explain how much he loved her. Because the idiot did. He was just too scared to see it.

Like Alex didn't have her own issues? She'd dated a ton of men she couldn't commit to, and they'd been a hell of a lot easier to handle than Hunter. Talk about difficult.

"You know, all this can keep. What did Jurek have to say?" It took a lot for her to squelch her overwhelming joy, but she did.

He opened his mouth, then closed it, eyeing her with suspicion. When she continued to wait calmly, he scowled. "Your brother discovered how Omaney and Wraith are

185

connected."

"Cole did?"

"Your uncle is pissed as hell at him. Cole broke into Omaney's house and found the information."

"Why would Uncle Max be upset about that?"

"Because Omaney was *in* the house at the time." Hunter gave her a ghost of a grin. "Your brother has balls, I'll give him that."

"I was right. Men are idiots." She fumed. And Max called *her* the troublemaker.

"So, what's the deal, Alex? What is it about your brother that puts you on the defensive?"

Before, she'd put him off. But now, everything changed. "Cole is...unique."

"Aren't we all?" he said dryly.

"Cole touches an object and knows things about the people who've handled it. It's called psychometry."

"No shit." Hunter looked impressed.

"Yeah. That's why he had to take off his glove at Omaney's warehouse. He was feeling for information."

Hunter whistled. "A handy talent to have." He grimaced. "And a curse."

"He's built some solid shields over the years, so he doesn't need to wear gloves all the time. But sometimes intense sensations overwhelm him. And in Omaney's office, we didn't want to leave any prints."

"Wonder what he saw when he latched onto me."

"Funny. He normally doesn't get anything off people."

Hunter's eyes widened. "No, but I was wearing my watch. He must have sensed something from that."

If the information had been enough to startle Cole, she'd bet it had something to do with her. Alex blanched.

Hunter apparently thought the same thing, for he chuckled. "I bet your brother caught an eyeful."

"That's not funny," she said on a groan.

"Trust me, it is. It also explains why he was so opposed to us spending any time together. And why he's been a royal pain in Jurek's ass, wanting to see for himself that you're okay."

"I'm glad you're enjoying this." Pleased that his sour mood seemed to have disappeared, she actually didn't mind his humor.

"Oh, I am." When he stopped laughing, he continued to explain Jurek's phone call. "Omaney took the bait. We're traveling tomorrow. I'll drive us to your place, where J.D. will pick us up in a limo and take us to a small airport in Brunswick. From there, we'll be flown to Wraith."

"And the auction."

He nodded. He studied her for a few moments, then patted his lap. "Come here, angel."

She would have balked at the command, but the tenderness behind it drew her. She settled on his lap and waited.

He kissed her, so gently she barely felt it. "Alex, I won't lie. I don't want you to go tomorrow." He put a hand over her lips when she would have argued. "I know. It's too late for you to back out. As much as Omaney wants me there, he wants you there as well. I get that. But I don't have to like it."

Hunter hugged her to him, tucking her head under his chin against his chest. She heard his heart beat, felt his breath go in and out of his body, and inhaled the pure, masculine scent of him. Suddenly, the excitement of being operational didn't matter as much as the fear of what might go wrong. What if something happened to Hunter on this mission? What if he was hurt, or worse, killed by those criminals?

"Hunter, I—"

"I'm scared for you, angel. I can't help it." He held her in his arms, and they sat quietly. "But I know you can handle yourself. I believe in you, Alex."

His words meant everything to her. "I believe in you, too." She leaned back to look at him, and the emotion in his gaze took her breath away.

"Remember what you said, angel. I'm your maniac."

"You want me to remember that?" she asked with a desperate laugh.

"Just remember I'm yours." He sighed. "And when this thing is over, you and I are going to seriously talk."

"So, Peter Omaney and Wraith are friends?" Alex asked the next day as she rode next to Hunter—dressed as Jed Black—in their limo. In another twenty minutes, they'd be at the airport, ready to go God-knew-where.

"Wraith, born Raymond Guest, was the son of a preacher. He grew up poor, abused, and unloved. I'm crying a river." He snorted.

"So he turned into an arms dealer, smuggler, and now human trafficker?"

"Bingo. Not sure on the details, but his initials match the ones in Omaney's files that J.D. was looking into. Now that we know the players, we can start changing the rules in this game. I can't wait to take these assholes down."

"Right, though I don't know I'd have put it the same way."

Ever since Hunter had assumed Jed Black's identity this morning, she'd sensed his energy skyrocket. Her own anticipation heightened, and she used the fear of the unknown to strengthen her resolve. She would help Hunter find Rebecca *and* keep an eye on him. "I still can't believe we found Wraith's client list. That's a huge plus. Congressman Ulie?" She still couldn't believe that name. Hell, she'd voted for him last year.

"Just goes to show that criminals come in all shapes and sizes."

"Great." She tugged at her short Nicole Miller day dress, glad of at least one tangible positive on this trip. A kick-ass wardrobe.

Hunter continued, eyeing her thighs with interest. "We also found out Omaney has a gambling problem. He never loses more than he can afford and always paid his debts. Except now we know that his debts weren't being paid by his diminishing trust fund, but by Guest. They've been in each other's pockets for years."

"So Guest keeps Omaney out of hock, and Omaney uses his legal connections and political friends to keep Guest out of the limelight. Talk about a perfect relationship." She started when Hunter ran a hand along the inside of her thigh. "Hunter," she breathed and glanced at the partition currently separating them from J.D.

"It's Jed, angel. Jed Black. Remember that. And whatever I do, just go along with it," he reminded her. "Jed Black is a real bastard. He's not above using you to further his own ends. I may have to get a little explicit around the others, and I just want you to know—"

"It's not you doing it. I know, Hunter." Alex leaned forward to kiss his cheek. Except he moved and met her mouth. His lips caressed, coaxed, and aroused her past reason in no time.

Alex was not by nature an exhibitionist. But it took her a moment to realize the partition had lowered, J.D. was laughing at her, and Hunter still had his hand between her legs.

Her cheeks burned, and she shoved at Hunter's immovable frame. He removed his hand, but not before he slid his fingers over her wet panties.

"I think this is going to work just fine," he said in a low voice.

"You two are convincing," J.D. added. "Better than Skinemax."

Alex pretended not to hear him, and she scowled at Hunter's satisfied grin. "Maniac."

"All yours, angel. Just you remember that."

"Ahem." J.D. cleared his throat. "Remember, *Jed*, your shoes are your lifeline. The transponder we're using is undetectable. All you have to do is plug it in and I'll sense it. Nothing can block that signal, trust me. Just find an outlet and you're golden."

Hunter tapped his shoe on the floor. "Will do."

"I packed another device for you, on the off chance you lose your shoes. It's in your shaving kit. And remember, keep the transponder. As soon as you have eyes on, plug it in again and push the button. When the small LED turns green, you'll know the cavalry is on its way."

Hunter nodded.

"Eyes on?" Alex asked.

"Eyes on Rebecca, the target," Hunter explained.

Alex thought it all sounded a little too James Bondish to her. "You're sure this will work? I'm not too happy about being stuck on Wraith's turf without someone knowing where we are." To her shock, in the mirror, J.D.'s eyes glowed a bright, neon blue for a second before dimming.

"Trust me, I'll find you. You could say electricity and I are best friends."

"Yeah. He's hell at parties," Hunter muttered. He leaned forward and closed the partition between them, ignoring J.D.'s snicker of laughter. "Now, angel, you're good to go. Right?"

"Right."

"Play your part, and we'll do just fine. Do not adlib it. I mean it."

He sounded hard and mean, and desire for him flared in an instant.

"Hell." Hunter took a deep breath and sighed. "Try not to distract me too much, okay? Omaney's going to be eyeing you like a piece of meat, and we definitely don't want to see you on the auction block. Remember, you've hooked Jed on that sweet ass of yours. He's going to stick to you like glue and rub it in Omaney's face. We just need to see Rebecca and the others, then give the team enough time to get to wherever we're going."

Alex did her best not to roll her eyes. They'd been over this a dozen times already. As he continued to warn her about everything and anything that could go wrong and what to do to fix things, she traced patterns over his hand, taken with the energy she could almost feel buzzing through his skin.

"You haven't heard a word I've said," he muttered. "Dammit, Alex—"

"I heard you. I heard you. Now relax. We have a job to do, so let's do it."

"We're here," J.D. said through the intercom. The car slowed and came to a stop. "Good luck."

The plane ride lasted an hour, but most of that had been

flying in circles. Even an inexperienced traveler like Alex knew when a plane changed direction several times. After the plane taxied and came to a complete stop, the silent guards who'd ridden with them escorted Alex and Jed outside to a dark SUV. Blindfolded, she and Jed rode for another forty-five minutes before being freed from their blindfolds. A guard escorted them out of the vehicle and to a mansion sitting in a tropical paradise. Beyond the house she could see snatches of ocean. Great, they were somewhere off the coast. So much for a best guess of their location. And still no sign of Peter Omaney. Though the guards mentioned Peter had been unavoidably detained, Alex had a bad feeling about his absence.

The front doors opened. "Welcome to Ray's Island," a swarthy man with dark hair and eyes commented, his gaze intense as he studied them both. He wore linen slacks and a silk, short-sleeved dress shirt that screamed money. "Please follow me. Joshua will have your things delivered to your room."

They followed him through several wide hallways. Alex's heels echoed against the gold-veined marble beneath her. Birds of paradise and bougainvillea peeked in at her through the open windows allowing a cool breeze to pass. Were it not for the circumstances surrounding their visit, Alex would have stood in awe of such beauty. Yet all she could think about were abused women probably caged like animals amidst this paradise.

"I'm Yasef. Should you need anything during your stay, feel free to ring for me. I am at your disposal," he said warmly, but Alex felt something hungry and dark through his eyes when they fixed on her. A shiver of foreboding unnerved her, and she took a step closer to Hunter.

Yasef led them to an outdoor patio full of guests—*male* guests. Their faces matched the detailed list of attendees she and Hunter had been given last night. And there was Ulie, that bastard. Hunter's solid hand on her back pulled her together, and she smiled at the surprised and appraising looks sent her way.

Yasef led them toward a man in the middle of the party. "Ray, your newest guests have arrived." Ray excused himself from his conversation and turned to them. The moment of truth.

Raymond Guest. Wraith.

Tall and slim, he possessed an innate grace she wouldn't have imagined in a murderer, thief, and slaver. His pale blond hair and light blue eyes twinkled merrily, startling her anew that someone so terrible could seem so handsome and happy. Though she'd seen a blurred photo of him at a much younger age, he still appeared the exact opposite of what she'd expected, and the knowledge threw her.

"Ray, this is Jed Black and his enchanting companion, Ms. Alexandra Tyrell," Yasef introduced.

Ray nodded, his gaze calculating yet approving. She watched as Jed did the same thing before reaching out to shake Ray's hand. The grip looked firm, but not overly so, and both men smiled, probably at the pleasure of meeting someone they considered an equal.

Then Ray turned to her. "Alex, may I call you that?" She nodded. "What a pleasure." He lifted her hand and kissed the back of it before letting her go. He did nothing improper, yet Alex had the uneasy sensation that he wanted to, which surprised her. With the unlucky harem at his disposal, why would he possibly want her? And where the hell was Peter?

Ray nodded politely. "You're quite lovely, Alex. You're a lucky man, Jed."

Jed pulled Alex closer to his side, his hand running over her hip with familiarity. "You have no idea," he murmured and kissed Alex's neck. He raised his hand to her ribcage, sitting right below her breast.

Alex smiled up at Jed, aware of the importance of this first meeting. *Play it cool and sophisticated, but show him part of that good girl lurking beneath that tight skirt,* Hunter had said. A good thing, since she couldn't control her blush at such public fondling.

"Luck's a funny thing," Ray said thoughtfully. "One minute it's there, and the next it's gone."

"Too true. That's why I like to leave very little to chance," Jed murmured.

Ray nodded. "I like the way you think, Jed. Perhaps that's why we've both been so successful for so long." After a moment, he turned a puzzled expression toward Yasef. "Where's Peter?"

Hunter answered him. "Peter never showed at the airport, but his guards told us he'd be joining us as soon as he'd taken care of some business."

"Ah." Ray nodded. A trio of men in designer suits motioned for his attention. "If you'll excuse me?"

"Please, don't let us keep you." Jed continued to hold her, his caresses growing bolder as the men around them gave her more and more attention. Ray frowned and left them. "I think we should find our room," Jed whispered into her ear as his hand roved over her bottom and pulled her into his erection.

"Good idea." *Get me away from these sharks.* She nipped his earlobe.

"Yasef," Hunter called to the man studying them both. "We'd like to see our room."

"Of course, Mr. Black. Right this way." He led them back through the house. They walked down the large main hallway and then turned left down a wing full of rooms.

"This is the south wing," Yasef informed them. "All of Ray's guests are in this wing of the house. In the east wing you'll find most of the festivities planned for this weekend. In the west wing are the kitchen and dining areas. And in the north wing are Ray's personal quarters. There's a small map in your room."

Yasef stopped at a door marked *Angel Suite*. "Ray thought you'd like this." He pushed the door open.

The ceiling had been painted a soft blue under a fresco of cupid's minions shooting naked men and women alike. Creamy silk paper covered the walls, over which several antique paintings of angels and saints sat. The floor was a soft, tan pebbled carpeting that complemented the room, and the only part of the room not covered with angelic decor.

A king-size bed and a matching dark-mahogany armoire and dresser completed the furnishings. All in all, the room spoke of decadence, which would have interested her more if she hadn't been so unnerved by her host.

"Cocktails will begin in an hour, dinner served soon after," Yasef said, looking at his watch. "Just go back to the main hallway and take a right. You'll hear everyone milling about by then." He smiled. His gaze moved over Alex like grimy hands. "Enjoy," he murmured and closed the doors behind him when he left.

Alex had no chance to speak before Hunter took her mouth in a possessive kiss.

Chapter Thirteen

Jed guided Alex toward the bathroom as he continued to kiss away her will to resist.

"How about a shower to cool us off, baby?" he said roughly. He entered the bathroom, closed and locked the door behind him, and mouthed, *"They're listening."* He pointed all around.

She nodded and played along with his mock seduction, moaning with him while he looked for electronic bugs.

He removed his belt and held it up in front of him. To her confusion, he held the belt up to first one wall, then another, running the belt over surfaces like a scanner. He stepped inside the shower and again searched for listening devices, she assumed. After checking everything, including the showerhead and drain, he gave her a thumbs up.

Hunter turned on the shower, then removed his shoes. Pushing apart the heel from his left shoe, he took out a tiny device and plugged it into an outlet. After a few seconds, he put it back in his shoe and locked the heel into place. He continued to undress and nodded at her to do the same. "We're clean."

Once naked, Alex followed him into the glass-walled haven. "Literally," she murmured as she stood under the water. When she realized Hunter stayed well away from the spray, she started in dismay. "What about your face? You shouldn't be in here."

"I just need to keep my eyes closed so my contacts don't fall out. The dye will keep, as will the prosthetics. This isn't my first job, Alex."

She flushed. No, it was hers. "So, now what?"

"Now I do what I've been needing to since we got on that damned jet and entered this house of sin," Hunter snarled. He pulled Alex to him and kissed her hungrily. "I need you."

Alex wrapped herself around him, and he groaned. His kissed his way down her body, paying special attention to her breasts.

"I love your nipples. They get so hard for me." He licked and sucked, until she nearly begged him to end it. But he wouldn't be rushed. By the time his lips again met hers, she could barely stand. Hunter lifted her up and braced her against the tiled wall. Then he lowered her body over his until she gloved him.

Alex threw back her head in ecstasy as Hunter took her. The cold Jed Black didn't exist in here with her. Hunter Greye claimed her. He possessed her and loved her until she cried out her release. As she clenched around him, he shuddered and poured into her on a groan.

After what felt like forever, Hunter unlocked her legs from behind his back and withdrew. He lowered her gently to the floor once more.

"I wanted to kill every one of those bastards for the way they looked at you," he said in a low voice. "You're mine."

She thrilled to hear him say it. He bent to clean her up, and once again she realized that, were it not for the Pill, she might become pregnant by this man. A sense of longing consumed her, adding yet another layer of confusion to this already complex play.

"You okay?"

I will be once I get my biological clock under control. "I'm great, now. So we can't talk in the bedroom safely, right?"

"No." He frowned. "And I've no doubt he's got cameras in there as well."

"How will we communicate? We can't keep running for the shower."

"No, but we'll make the most of it when we do. It'll be easy enough to spot his cameras. J.D.'s a pain in the ass, but his spy gear is top rate." Hunter pointed at his belt. "I can find anything electronic with that." He paused. "Any thoughts on Omaney?"

"No. He should have been here. Do you think he backed off because he knows who we are?" She lowered her voice. "Did you see the room they put us in? The *Angel* Suite? Because I'm a Sainte? Coincidence?"

"Believe it or not, yes. If Ray had any idea of who you really were, he'd have killed us before we got on the plane. Trust me, I know how this guy works." He slicked her hair back. "Don't worry. The transponder's working. Even now, J.D.'s pinpointed our location and a crew is standing by." He sighed. "Now, as much as I'd rather spend the rest of the night in here with you, we need to dry off and dress. We also have to play to the cameras. But you know, I'm a savvy guy. We won't give Ray too much of a show."

After they dried off, they entered the main room again. Hunter stilled for a moment, then angled himself between her and the dresser. At his nod, she dropped her towel and redressed quickly, in clean, dry panties this time. Hunter didn't move until she'd covered herself, though he quickly reverted to Jed. He made crude remarks about Alex's sexual acrobatics and alluded to her heavenly mouth while he subtly swept the room with his belt buckle in the palm of his hand. Then he turned to the ornament on top of the mirror above the dresser and smiled.

"If you want to see more, you have to deal with me, Ray. We can talk about it after dinner."

Jed took Alex in his arms again and kissed her like a starving man, his hands fondling her intimately. When he let her go, he winked at the camera.

Ray waited for them in the dining hall with the others. He kept his irritation hidden under a bright smile while he plotted Black's destruction.

He'd watched Black and Alex leave earlier, had seen the sexual touches and the knowing glint in the man's eyes. Excusing himself, Ray had hurried back to his study to watch them through one of his many hidden cameras.

He'd been more than disappointed when they left the bedroom for the lavatory. As much as Ray liked control over others, he hadn't wanted to see such base human functions on-screen, so he'd refrained from putting cameras in his bathrooms.

When they returned to the bedroom, Ray had seen the satisfied look on the bastard's face and knew that he'd just had sex with Alex in the bathroom. Ray hadn't expected Black's bold announcement directed right at the hidden camera though.

He smiled at something Congressman Ulie said while his mind dwelled on his perfect angel. Peter's picture hadn't done her justice. In the flesh, Alexandra Tyrell spoke to him on another level entirely. She made him crave, the epitome of temptation, and he realized his father's words were finally coming to fruition. The demon son would finally fall, then ascend through an angel's eyes. With Alex, Ray could finally complete his life's work with *Corruption of the Saint.*

He exhaled a soft sigh of satisfaction as Black and Alex finally joined them in the dining room. Alex looked breathtaking. The patterned, skintight dress in bright hues enhanced her golden skin. And the color of her eyes... *Absolutely magnificent.*

He imagined her dressed in white, her wings spread out behind her as he dominated her body, mind, and soul. He loved that painting. It defined him.

As ordered, Yasef seated Alex between Ray and Black.

"I hope you feel well rested," Ray said and watched her blush becomingly.

Jed's obnoxious laughter boomed. "Hell, Ray. Rest was the last thing on our minds, right, baby?" Ray stared at the man in distaste; Jed Black had no class. Alex, he noted, glanced at Black with disgruntlement.

Perhaps she wouldn't be so hard to steal from Black after all. The man must have been good in bed, or Alex wouldn't still be with him. As much as Ray contemplated the ethereal, he knew flesh and blood women had needs. Just like the men at this table had needs.

As everyone sampled their lobster bisque, Ray studied Alex and her present companion. From a purely aesthetic viewpoint, he had to admit that together they looked spectacular. Alex's light hair and golden skin complemented Jed's black hair and darker complexion. The couple glowed with health, and both appeared to be in top physical shape. Ray's gaze lingered over Alex's curves, approving such vibrancy.

"So, Alex, how did you meet Jed?" he asked, curious to hear it from her.

"She met me at Seneca's, right before I stole her from Peter," Jed answered him.

"I believe I was speaking to the lady." Ray frowned. The warm smile Alex rewarded him with lifted his spirits, as well as other lagging parts of his body. Jed shrugged and turned his attention to the oil magnate next to him.

"It's like he said, Ray. Is it all right if I call you Ray?" Alex asked softly.

He placed a hand over hers on the table. Pure heat generated at the contact, and Ray dropped his hand. "That's fine, Alex. Everyone calls me Ray."

She smiled, disarming him again. "I met Jed at Seneca's, like he said. Peter and I had spent some time together. He seems like a wonderful man. I do hope to see him later. I really liked him, but I can't explain it. The minute I saw Jed, it was like magic. He kissed me, and it was over." Ray noticed that she didn't look pleased over the admission.

"So long as you're happy." Ray sampled his bisque, but he didn't taste it. Every part of him fixated on Alexandra Tyrell.

"Ray? Where are all of your female guests?" Alex looked around the table.

"I'm afraid this is a business trip for most of my friends. Though you haven't seen their wives and girlfriends, they're here." He smiled. "You'll probably see some of them tomorrow night at the party. Unfortunately, business sometimes comes first."

Alex nodded. "I know. I model, and after this weekend I have to hurry back to Savannah to start my shoot for *Chic* magazine."

"How wonderful! I'm sitting next to someone who's going to be the next face of the year, I'm sure. I know a lot of people in the industry. You have the face and body of a woman destined to go places." He gauged her reaction and saw her hanging onto his every word, her body turned from Black.

Marie Harte

Alex blushed, and Ray's body reacted violently. He carefully readjusted the napkin on his lap and scooted closer to the table. As he did so, Jed refocused his attention on Alex. The man didn't look happy.

"Ray," a tall Texan down the table called out. "When are we going to get down to business?"

The rest of the table grew silent waiting for Ray's response. Even Jed turned his attention to his host.

"In due time, Hal," Ray chided the man. "Enjoy your dinner first. And rest assured that, after tonight, you'll better understand the details of just what I can offer you."

Hal nodded. Conversation resumed around the table. The rest of the meal passed in surprising normalcy, as if he hosted a dinner party for civilized men, and not a pack of dogs waiting for him to throw them a bone.

Ray contained his disgust and encouraged conversation. He didn't much care for any of the men around him. Once again, he wondered about Peter. His friend had finally called and was on his way, but his vague excuse for missing the jet bothered Ray. Almost as much as Jed Black's continued displays of possession annoyed him. The way Black's large hands continued to caress and fondle Alex during dinner had not only offended him, but caused him to feel protective of the young woman.

She deserved better than the animal mauling her. Ray would never do such a thing. In the privacy of his own bedroom, touching would of course be a necessity. But to display it so openly curdled his stomach, as did most of the men he'd invited to his home.

Hypocrites, the lot of them. Black at least remained true to himself. He came across as a man who took what he wanted, and he did. Like Ray, who knew exactly what he wanted out of

202

life—redemption. A surcease from the unending agonies of guilt and rage that consumed him between bouts of mania.

During those manic phases, Ray reveled in women and drugs and death. He especially liked killing, and he made no bones about it. The rush of ending a life aroused him more than any woman ever had...until Alex.

As she talked to her lover and the senator across the table from her, Ray wondered if she knew what Jed did for a living. The innocent woman she appeared would balk at the idea of women being drugged and sold as slaves. His angel would shun Black the minute she learned what a villain he truly was. She would, of course, make an exception for Ray. Like that unexplainable lust that had first drawn her to Black, Alex would be unable to stop herself from surrendering to him. A woman's place—obedient, God-fearing, and pliable.

The meal drew to a close. Yasef leaned down to whisper in his ear, "Peter's arrived. Should I direct everyone to the green room once they're finished?"

Ray nodded, relieved Peter had finally come. He sat back and waited, curious to see how Black would handle Alex.

"Honey, you go on back to the room," Jed murmured to her. "It's time for business. Don't worry. When I'm done, I'm sure I'll be ready for you again." He leaned close and kissed her full on the mouth, heedless of the envious stares around him.

Releasing her, he turned and cast a hard look on the others staring at them, forcing them to look away. Possessive and base, but very effective. He acted like a dog marking its territory.

Alex blushed. "Yes, Jed." She turned and gifted Ray with a shy smile. "Thank you for a lovely meal. I hope your business proves fruitful tonight."

"Oh, I'm sure it shall." Ray stood when she did and bowed

a good night. He watched her leave, and turned back to see Black studying him without expression.

"I think once the meeting is over, you and I will have something to talk about, hmm?" Jed drawled.

"Perhaps." Ray shrugged, then turned to the others. "Gentlemen? Follow me please. It's time to get down to business."

Alex walked down the corridor to her room and almost ran into Peter Omaney.

"Peter," she said, startled. "I missed you."

Peter looked harried. His cheek and jaw appeared bruised, his lower lip looked swollen, and he had dark circles under his eyes.

"Are you okay?"

He continued to look at her, saying nothing. Her unease grew, especially when he smiled. There was no joy in his expression, but a feral amusement. *At her expense?*

"Peter?" He was really creeping her out.

"Going to bed?" He licked his lips, dragging his tongue across a spot of dried blood.

"Yes. I'm really tired. It's been a long day."

"And it's bound to get longer." Peter shocked her by wrapping a hand around her throat. But he didn't squeeze. He trailed his fingers down her chest, into the valley between her breasts. "Jed's no saint, is he? Not like you. Sweet dreams, Alex."

The minute he turned away, she hurried down the hall and threw herself into the room. She locked the door behind her and leaned back against the door, her heart pounding. *Oh my God.*

He knows.

Jed Black sat with eight other guests and waited for Ray to begin. He couldn't wait for the cavalry to arrive. Four of these assholes had influential ties to the government. The other four had money coming out their ears. Only a handful were currently under investigation for suspected criminal activity, but mostly white-collar crap, nothing so vile as slave trading.

After a half hour of bullshit, Ray called the group to order and everyone took seats in his large media room. Peter Omaney walked in behind the others and sat next to Hunter in the back. After directing a grim smile his way, Peter nodded to Ray. *Shit.* What the hell did that mean? Hunter forced himself not to tense while he mentally prepared for the worst. He relaxed when the guards at the doors remained at ease, and Ray began to speak.

Ray stood, confident and controlled. "I appreciate your patience, my friends. Before we begin, I'd like to reiterate that security is as tight as a drum. I know a few of you have expressed concern about new faces, but I can assure you this is a private auction. Everyone present has been thoroughly searched, as has their luggage. The house is resistant to outside tampering, electronic and otherwise. Even if you still had your cell phones, you'd be unable to get a signal."

True, unless J.D. Morgan designed your transmitter. Hunter ignored several glances in his direction and raised a brow at Ray, aware that he—Jed Black—had caused more than a few concerns with the others.

"Excellent. Now then, let's get on with it, shall we?" Ray nodded to Yasef, who dimmed the lights and began punching buttons on a small remote.

At the front of the room, blue velvet curtains parted to

reveal a large white screen. It flickered to life, revealing a black background.

"What you are going to see next is just an example of what Plezure can do, in the right formulaic state. We've been developing a new concentration, and this latest batch seems to work best."

Numbers counted down until a picture appeared. A naked woman lay bound on a bed. She looked pale and scared. Tears fell down her cheeks and multiple bruises marred her skin. It wasn't Rebecca, but he recognized the female. Hunter's stomach rolled. Victoria Pinello, the daughter of an evangelical holy roller, had been abducted three months ago. Her body had been found floating off the coast a month after she'd disappeared. Police chalked it up to a random crime. Now Hunter knew better.

"Some of you may recognize Victoria from her father, Vincent Pinello." Several of the men murmured in surprise. "Victoria was a Yale grad and a major follower in her father's footsteps. She helped raise millions for his church in the years she spent working with him. Like I told you before, I've acquired only the best and the brightest for you gentlemen. No street whores or drugged-out vermin."

God forbid we don't have the best for this lot. Hunter deliberately relaxed his grip on the arms of his chair.

"Sophistication, purity, intelligence, and beauty." Ray nodded. "As you can see, Victoria isn't eager to perform. Not until we give her some of this."

The woman struggled, rubbing her wrists raw. She cried and begged to be let go. Then Yasef, the bastard, injected her with a syringe. Ten minutes later, the woman eased into anything he wanted. Everyone watched the duration of the picture. A half hour later, Victoria stared sightlessly at the ceiling over her bed. Yasef had cut her throat after cutting her in several other places.

Hunter prayed Yasef hadn't treated the others like this. The psychotic bastard.

Congressman Ulie huffed his displeasure. "Hell, Ray. I'm not interested in sullied trash. For what I'm paying, I expect perfection."

"Of course not, Bill. Victoria was a test. She served her purpose. The women we now have for sale are clean, unmolested, and devoid of any bruising but the emotional toll their stay has brought them. Many have been drugged over time to keep them docile, preventing any harm."

Several of the men around him nodded.

"Good, good." Ulie, the prick, looked pleased.

"Now, I realize several of you don't have the facilities to keep and maintain the girls, so I've decided to offer my services. A housekeeping service, if you will. Arrangements may be made after the auction."

"So you have them in house?" Hunter asked in a low voice.

"Of course," Ray answered. "I keep them close and constantly monitored. I wouldn't sell you tainted product."

"'Course not," Hal, sitting in the front, added. "Been dealing with Ray for years. He's aboveboard."

"Thank you, Hal."

The lovefest sickened him. A few more men asked questions, details about pedigrees, finances, ages, and more, until Ray held up a hand.

"Gentlemen, please. I think the best way to proceed is to take you to them."

Hunter's pulse leapt.

"This way, please."

He moved to follow the others to the door when Peter held him back. "What?" Hunter growled.

"You and I have to talk."

"Not now, Pete. We've just gotten to the good part." Hunter grinned through his teeth. "Take your hand away, or I'll break it off."

Peter quickly removed his hand, and Hunter noticed bruises over his knuckles. To his surprise, he noted several more under some makeup that didn't quite match Peter's skin tone.

Peter glanced around him, and seeing no one about, said in a low voice, "Fine. Follow Ray and the others. But meet me in the dining hall afterward. It's about Alex, and it's important."

Hunter wanted to blow him off, but mention of Alex caught his attention. "I'll be there." He hurried out the door and caught the tail end of the group meandering outside. God willing, he'd see Rebecca passed out and untouched, oblivious to this nightmare. Because the sooner he rescued her and took Alex out of this evil place, the better.

Chapter Fourteen

An hour and a half later, Alex still couldn't sleep. Pretending to be calm while she wanted to run after Hunter was killing her. Hell, she couldn't even pace out her nervousness. Mindful of the cameras, she pretended to sleep in the sexy lingerie someone had packed for her. She had a feeling J.D. had packed their suitcases, since he'd given her a wicked smile when he'd handed her the bag earlier. His penchant for silk and lace definitely called for a sit down.

The white teddy and silk white wrap that came to mid-thigh were not helping her to feel invulnerable. All she needed were fuzzy heels to complete the outfit.

Nervous, she tossed again, glad for the room's darkness, at least.

He knew. Somehow, Peter knew. The question then became, how much did he know, and how had he found out? The chance remained that Hunter's cover would hold. Jed Black had been honed over years. Unlike Alexandra Tyrell, who'd been crafted a few days ago and didn't have much in the way of background other than what had been recently created for her.

They still had that device in Hunter's shaving kit, the one that would call the troops in. But, until they found Rebecca, they couldn't afford to blow their cover, or whatever of it remained. Wracking her nerves to decide what to do, she nearly jumped out of her skin when the sound of a key in the doorknob scraped. Quickly sitting up, she turned on the light beside the bed and shrugged into the wrap she'd laid next to her. Not that it did much to cover her, but it would shield her a little from the cameras.

The knob turned, and she waited anxiously to share her news. She'd never before wanted *a shower* so much.

Except Peter stood in the doorway.

He closed the door behind him and leaned back on it. "Your boyfriend is otherwise occupied, Alex. That is your real name, isn't it?"

"Peter? Are you all right? You don't look well."

He looked better than he had when she'd last seen him. He must have doctored his face to hide the trauma. "I'm a lot better than you're going to be." He stepped forward, his gaze lingering on her breasts. "So sweet. Too bad you're not who you say you are. Then again, it really doesn't matter. One way or the other, you're going to tell me what you know. I can be nice, or I can be nasty. Which do you want, sweetheart?" He sneered and raced through the buttons on his shirt. "I'm all for nasty."

Alex didn't move. What would Hunter do in a situation like this? He'd handle it. Plain and simple. In this world of danger and make-believe, control would win in the end. And she still held that psychic ace in the hole.

The panic she'd initially felt faded. Calm purpose took over. "What do you think you know?" she asked coolly and crossed her arms under her breasts, aware that she enhanced her cleavage by doing so.

He licked his lips and fixated on her chest. "I know your name is Alexandra Sainte. You work for a private investigation firm. Probably tied to the government. They're just itching to take us down." He tossed his shirt to the floor and paused at the buckle on his belt. More bruises scraped along his ribs. "You don't look scared. Why is that?"

"You're not so scary." She shrugged. "I'm more worried about what Black will do if he finds out."

Peter regarded her with skepticism. "Do you honestly expect me to believe he doesn't already know?"

"Do you honestly think I'd still be alive if he knew? For all that Jed has a fierce reputation, even he can fall prey to that monster between his legs." She gave Peter a cold smile. "You all do."

Peter's eyes narrowed. "You little bitch." Then he laughed, surprising her. "You and Ray were made for each other. Amazing what a man will do for a piece of ass, he's always told me. And he's right. Mr. Bad Ass terrorist taken in by a Fed. I can't wait to see his face when Ray tells him."

"So you've already told Ray who I am?" *Please say no. Then again, if he hasn't, the camera has already ruined my shot at pretending. Shit.*

"Not yet. You're going to ease my way into his good graces. *Corruption of the Saint*, literally. You know something, Alex? Your asshole friends almost got me. But a friend tipped me off." He gently stroked his cheek and some makeup rubbed away. She could see the purpling bruise beneath. "They didn't expect me to escape."

"What friends are you talking about?"

"That's right. Stick to your script." Peter unbuckled his belt and unbuttoned his trousers. When he slid the zipper down, Alex steeled her mind and shifted the covers from her lower body. Peter already stood too close. But she wanted to be on her feet before he took the last few steps separating them.

Peter stuck his hand in his pants and squeezed himself.

Alex wanted to look anywhere but at him, but she kept her gaze centered on his lust-filled face.

"Come here, you little bitch. On your knees," he said thickly.

"Watch who you call a bitch," Alex murmured before she stepped closer and rammed her knee into his groin.

Peter tried to avoid her, but, already banged up, he shifted too late. On a groan, he clutched himself and fell to the ground.

Alex followed with a kick to his ribs and one to his face.

Before she could grab the lamp to knock him senseless, the door burst open and a guard shot her, right in the neck.

Alex gasped at the prick of pain and felt for blood. Her fingers found a small dart. Not good.

Fearful she would pass out before she could escape, Alex sent the guards into the walls with a flick of her wrist and her will. A sudden fog pressed all around her, and she forced one step after another out the door.

She made it a few feet down the hallway when another prick of pain hit her shoulder. Dizzy, Alex fell hard on her hands and knees. But before she could trace the gold vein on the marble rising to meet her face, blackness overtook her, and she saw nothing more.

Hunter experienced an odd sense of lightheadedness as he stared down at an unconscious Rebecca Mitchell. He wavered on his feet and shook his head. Bracing a hand on the wall, it took a moment before he regained his equilibrium.

He sensed trouble for Alex. Perhaps Peter had gone to Alex when Hunter hadn't shown for their meeting. Then again, several of Ray's guests had stayed behind to sample the merchandise before buying. Hunter scowled down at the syringe in his hand, one of many Ray had handed out. A shot of whatever the hell it contained would rouse Rebecca.

Not likely, since he wanted her quiet and easily managed. Thanks to soundproofed walls, Hunter couldn't hear the nightmare outside, nor could anyone hear him. A glance at the lone covered window on the door assured him of privacy.

A light flared on the slim phone mounted to the wall next to the door. Ray wanting him, maybe? Peter demanding his presence?

Hunter took a deep breath, then exhaled before answering. "Yeah?"

"It's me." J.D.'s voice carried softly over the phone. "Just returning your call." Hunter had recently plugged in the transponder and pressed the button. "Don't ask how I did it, just accept my genius and gimme the deets."

After explaining their arrival and Omaney's odd appearance, Hunter quickly sketched a rough picture of the mansion's layout and security, as well as the guesthouse's positioning in relation to the grounds and the guards.

After a few moments of silence, J.D. informed him of the extraction team's timeline. J.D. had bypassed some electronic security guarding the actual island, but he still had a few hurdles to overcome. Between his efforts and the logistics to get the rest of the team into place, he figured another half hour before the shit hit the fan.

Just enough time to find Alex, grab Rebecca, and haul ass into the surrounding jungle north of the estate.

"You better be damn sure you know what you're doing," Hunter growled.

"Have a little faith."

Hunter hung up, not as reassured as he should have been. Omaney's late arrival still bothered him, as did his reasons for wanting a powwow. J.D., up to speed on everything, had no idea what had delayed Omaney's arrival to the island. He swore Buchanan's team worked hand-in-hand with them on everything, so he didn't think Max, Cole, or Thorne had interfered.

A glance at Rebecca showed her breathing deep and even. Hunter didn't want to leave her alone, but an urgency gnawed at him to find Alex. Change in plan.

Hunter injected Rebecca with the serum. "Come on, dammit. Wake up."

After a few moments, her eyelids fluttered. It took several minutes before she showed an awareness of her surroundings. She screamed.

Thank God for soundproofing. "I don't have time for this." The need to protect Alex grew. "Enough," Hunter growled and leaned close.

Rebecca shut up on a squeak. Surprisingly, she looked little worse for wear.

"Keep your mouth shut and listen. I'm here on behalf of your parents. We're going to bust you and the others out of here in..." he paused to look at his watch, "...another twenty-five minutes. I have to find my partner. Until then, you're going to be alone. But I don't want you unprotected."

Hunter slipped a gun out from the back of his trousers. He showed her the safety, ejected the clip, and showed her the bullets before shoving it back and loading the weapon. "Locked and loaded. All you have to do is point and shoot." He started to hand it to her, then stopped. "Don't shoot me. This isn't a game. We can't alert security to any of this yet. As far as anyone outside this room knows, I'm screwing your brains out." He grimaced.

Tears fells down her cheeks. In the dim light, she looked like Alex, and his heart turned over. "Dammit, don't cry. Come on, honey. You have to be strong, just a little while longer." At his words, she sniffled and dried her eyes. "I know you can shoot. Your father used to take you to the Foreman Firing range when you were just a kid. He used to call you Dead-Eye." Harlan had given them details to assure Rebecca of their identity in the event they found her.

Her eyes widened. "Oh my God! My father did send you!"

"Yeah, now remember, this thing is loaded." He handed her the pistol and stepped toward the door. "Lie back in that bed after I'm gone and pretend you're traumatized. Not that much of a leap, eh? Keep the gun close by, but *don't* leave this room. There are still guards outside, and they're armed. The team coming to collect you will be looking for you in this spot."

"Okay, okay. I'm good. I'll wait." She spoke too quickly, and Hunter could see her struggling to remain calm.

"I'm going to find Alex and bring that damned woman back here. If I'm not back by the time they come to get you, something's wrong. Let them know."

"I will. They're coming though, right?"

Hunter grinned. "Yes, they are. And trust me when I say Omaney and the rest of these assholes are gonna feel it when we're through."

Hunter didn't like the emptiness in the halls of the mansion. A cool breeze swept the scent of flowers and sea salt through the causeways. Not one guard stepped out to meet him. None of the other guests lurked about, no doubt too busy making deals with Ray.

The need for vengeance rode him hard. He hurried back to his suite, only to find the door broken and blood on the floor. Not enough to indicate a terminal loss, but smudges of dark red stained the floor in spots, amping his adrenaline. If anything happened to Alex, he'd kill whoever had touched her.

Several footsteps echoed in the hallway, drawing nearer to his room. His fingers itched for a gun. Unfortunately, he'd given the only weapon he'd had to Rebecca. At least it would keep her safe. He glanced at his watch.

Fifteen more minutes until backup.

Yasef entered with half a dozen guards surrounding him. None of them appeared armed. "Ray would like to see you in his study."

"In a minute." As he looked at Yasef, he could only picture the deviant abusing Victoria. Between her legs, over her slim, helpless body...

Rage consumed him. Adrenaline increased his alertness, and his speed took the others by surprise. In seconds, he'd knocked one of the guards unconscious and disabled another by breaking his jaw

The remaining four guards closed in on him while Yasef watched with a grim smile. Needing to remain in control and unhampered, Hunter swiftly broke one guard's knee and kicked another in the face. He didn't stop until the men around him lay on the ground, unmoving. Once done with them, he turned on Yasef. The bastard held a pistol, but Hunter was already moving. With his keener than average eyesight, he watched Yasef's finger tighten on the trigger and shifted out of the way. He felt a burn across his shoulder and kept moving. He knocked into Yasef, taking the man off his feet.

In short order, he wrapped a hand around Yasef's neck and grabbed the gun. Hunter stood and yanked Yasef to his feet by his hair. Forcing the smaller man to walk ahead of him, he said, "I'm ready. Let's go find your boss."

After several twists and turns, Yasef led Hunter to a door inside Ray's personal quarters. The gunmetal gray door stood out in the room because it had no handle, and its cold exterior looked incongruous with the tropical-themed suite. Coral, green, and ivory decorated everything from the bedspread to the curtains to the chair cushions. The room might as well have been for a guest, because nothing personal indicated the room was even in use. No speck of dust or wrinkle marred the room's perfection.

"Only Ray can unlock it," Yasef said in a low voice.

At his words, the door *snicked* and opened. Hunter looked at Yasef, the urge to kill strong. But Victoria hadn't had it so easy. Neither would Yasef. A quick death wouldn't hurt nearly as much as a lifetime behind bars. Shoving the man ahead of him through a dark corridor, he followed and entered a large, windowless room.

One half of the room looked like a miniature art exhibit. Several paintings lined a blood-red wall, each lit by a warm light. Angels and demons seemed a common motif. A couch faced away from him toward the paintings, presumably to allow Ray to absorb his intimidating art. Several glass-encased sculptures and a large water fountain covering the side wall from ceiling to floor dominated the rest of the space. The sounds of trickling water should have been soothing. Yet the serenity of this room seemed somehow forced.

Ray sat across from Peter Omaney, an expansive mahogany desk between them. Peter had been worked over, no doubt about it. Before this, his bruises had been concealed, but now blood trickled from his mouth, and he sported a black eye. The way Ray rubbed his hand made Hunter wonder if he'd had anything to do with Peter's new injuries.

"We have a few things to discuss," Ray said in a calm voice.

"Yeah, we do." Hunter shoved Yasef to his knees and aimed the gun at his head. "This asshole and a few of his friends tried to kill me."

"Tsk tsk." Ray frowned at his man. "Your orders were to bring him here. Not to harm him."

"But, Ray, he's one of them. Like her," Yasef protested.

Hunter strove to remain outwardly calm. One of them? He had a bad feeling his and Alex's covers had been blown.

"What the hell are you talking about?" he growled at Yasef, who slowly rose to his feet. "Ray and I have business to discuss. Breaking into my room? Trying to strong-arm me? What the fuck did you think you were doing?" He didn't have to pretend his rage. Turning to Ray, he snarled, "Where's Alex? She wasn't where I left her." His heart raced. *Please, God. She's not dead. She can't be.*

"Didn't you see her? She's right over there." Ray pointed to the couch.

Hunter left Yasef and hurried to the couch. Hidden by the high back, she lay peacefully on the cushions. To his relief, she didn't appear harmed. Wearing that racy negligee, she looked an awful lot like the woman in the painting centered on the wall in front of her. Without meaning to, he glanced from it to her. *Corruption of the Saint.* The damned thing gave him the creeps.

"Yes, incredible likeness, isn't it?" Ray smiled, but Peter frowned.

A thought struck him. Rebecca had been wearing a similar white slip, and she looked a lot like Alex. "Shit. They're all like the woman in the painting, aren't they? Every damned one of your women looks like her."

"Exactly. I've been searching for her for a long, long time. And you've brought her to me."

"She's a Fed," Omaney spat. "You can't keep her, Ray. You have to kill her. She's a liability."

"What do you think, Jed?" Ray asked softly.

Shit. "If this is your way of trying to take her for free, forget it. We trade. You want her, I'll give her to you. For a price." He walked around the couch, keeping himself between Alex and the others. "This Fed bullshit isn't flying."

"It's not bullshit. I have a source at Westlake," Peter insisted.

Dammit. That hit at the docks and his source have to be tied. "And what the hell is Westlake?"

"A private contractor for the government. They work hand in hand with the Feds on everything. A friend of mine told me Alex wasn't who she said she was. Turns out, she works for another firm, also in bed with the Bureau."

Hunter shook his head in denial.

Ray spoke before Peter could. "Funny. The great Jed Black taken in by a government agent. Then again, we don't really know you very well, do we, Jed? You surface every few years and do a good bit of business. Interesting you've never had any run-ins with the law." Ray toyed with a silver letter opener that resembled a miniature blade.

"Why are we asking twenty questions? Let's kill this scum and get back to business," Yasef seethed. He took a step toward Hunter, and Hunter raised his gun, silently praying for the deviant to attack.

Two shots rang out, and Yasef fell to the floor, dead. In one hand, Ray held his letter opener, in the other a nine-millimeter Beretta.

"I loved that man." Ray shook his head. "But he really would have come to a bad end if I hadn't saved him from himself. I'm so sorry, Peter, but he killed Sarah last night. Without my authority, I might add. I fear Yasef's demons were too much, even for a saint to fix." Ray glanced at the couch.

To Hunter's horror, Alex moaned and stirred behind him.

"She's coming around," Peter said, his voice oddly somber. "I'd like to see Sarah, if you wouldn't mind."

"Of course. I cleaned her up and left her in her room for you." Ray's voice gentled. "I'm sorry, Peter. I know you were fond of her." He buzzed his friend out the door, and they waited in silence while Omaney left.

"Poor man. He was taken with Sarah. They really did make a pretty pair." Ray sighed, then raised his gun at Hunter. "And now it's just you and me. Tell me, Mr. Greye, just what you hoped to accomplish by all this?"

Hunter didn't bat an eye. *I have a source at Westlake,* Omaney had said. Dammit all. His cover compromised and Alex's safety at risk, Hunter had no other choice but to take Ray out the hard way. "When did you know?"

Ray grimaced. "Not soon enough. I would never have invited you here were I in full faculty of the truth. Peter told me the minute I returned from our short tour. I'd wondered which woman you were sent for, and when you asked for Rebecca, I knew." He shifted his gun from Hunter to where Alex had risen from the couch to blink warily at both men. "I won't miss. Don't make me hurt her, Mr. Greye. Toss the gun."

Hunter didn't hesitate. He put the safety on and threw the gun toward Ray.

"Good."

Hunter blocked Alex by taking a step in front of her. He advanced in Ray's direction to cut down on Ray's line of sight, but he stopped when Ray aimed at his head.

"Not too close, my lethal friend. I applaud you for using Black as a cover. Ingenious. Tell me, does Jed Black really exist?"

"Yeah, and he's going to be plenty pissed when he hears he's been played. But if this works the way it's supposed to, not only will we have the infamous Wraith in custody, but a lead on Jed Black as well. Two for the price of one." At least he could keep Jed Black's identity secret.

"Very clever indeed." Ray walked around his desk, keeping a healthy distance between himself and Hunter. "You know you're not going to escape alive."

"I knew the risks when I volunteered for this. But you're not getting away either."

"Oh, but I am. I have redemption within my grasp for the first time in my life. That painting behind you? It's called *Corruption of the Saint*. The artist is unknown, but the painting dates back to 1435. My father gave it to me when I was just a young man. You see, he knew what he'd made when he impregnated my mother. Tainted by sin, he expelled his evil deeds into his only son. But that same evil lived on in me. The only way to purge myself is to accept what I am."

"And what's that? A murderer? A kidnapper and rapist?"

"All that, and more. But I can be saved. I just needed the right woman to give me respite. Alex can do that. She's the real thing. I saw what she can do. She's my ethereal angel, come to save me."

The crazed glow in Ray's light blue eyes scared the hell out of him. The bastard actually believed all this crap about sin and redemption. Hunter had to keep this killer as far from Alex as possible.

"She kept Peter away from her with no more than a wave of

221

her hand," Ray continued, his voice whisper-soft. "Her wings are there. We just can't see them. With her by my side, I can finally break free from what he made me." His eyes glittered with fanaticism and a hint of sadness.

Ray tightened his grip on his gun. "But you're going to have to go. I'm only sorry you touched her first. She was never yours to begin with. Alex, my dear, get down."

"Hunter," Alex screamed as Hunter rushed Ray to knock the gun aside.

The shot hit him hard, like a punch in his shoulder. Before Ray could fire again, a raging alarm sounded.

In the split second Ray's attention wavered, Hunter scrambled for the gun. Before he tore it away, another shot went off. Ray, despite his size, was deceptively strong. It took more effort than Hunter would have thought to wrench away the firearm.

"Why is my alarm blaring? What did you do?" Ray shrieked as Hunter threw him up against the wall, pinning him there by his shoulders.

"I'm crushing your world, you freak. You're done, Ray. Now the big, bad Wraith is nothing more than what he's always been—a pathetic little sinner with a daddy complex."

Unadulterated rage turned Ray's face into a demonic mask of hate. He landed a kick at Hunter's thigh that brought Hunter to his knees. The accompanying dizziness forced Hunter to acknowledge he'd been hit with that second shot and that Ray knew it. Ray took advantage, digging his fingers into Hunter's shoulder as well, as if to rip Hunter's flesh apart. The pain shocked him in its intensity, but the spots in his vision worried him. If he passed out, he'd leave Alex at this fuck's mercy.

"Stop it, Ray," Alex's voice pierced the alarm.

They both turned to see her stumble around the couch.

"Stay back," Hunter warned.

"Come to me, my angel," Ray crooned. "Save me from my sins."

"Oh, I will," Alex promised. She held her head in one hand. In the other, she motioned to one of the guns and it flew through the air to her.

"A miracle," Ray breathed and squeezed Hunter's wound hard enough to bring tears to his eyes.

Hunter blinked to clear his vision, but what happened next took a minute to register. He heard a noise, saw Alex's face crumple with worry. Then she was shoving Ray off him and to the floor.

"He's gone. Hunter, stay with me."

"Not...going...anywhere..."

"You're mine, remember that."

Hers, always. He closed his eyes with a smile on his face.

Epilogue

"You know, it's been three months and we still haven't had our talk," Alex said and kissed Hunter. They sat in her office, she in his lap, and he in her desk chair. He still hadn't said those three little words she wanted so badly to hear.

"I'm not sure this thing is going to hold us," Hunter muttered, looking down at the creaking monstrosity that would be coming with her.

"It's great. Just think how terrific it's going to look in our new office." Alex grinned.

"As long as you're behind the desk, I'll agree to anything." Hunter still reminded her, at least once a day, that he'd found her in Ray's clutches. He'd saved her, before she'd saved him—which she wouldn't let *him* forget.

"Well, I'll admit the need to prove myself is gone. I saved the day, if you think about it." She toyed with his hair, liking it longer. Her hero, so dark and dangerous. Until he smiled. He smiled a lot since they'd let him out of the hospital. And he had a grin on his face every night when they climbed into bed together, and after...

He shifted under her, and the feel of his hard body caging hers made her flush. He pulled her more firmly over him and laughed. Nuzzling her throat, he teased, "What's wrong, angel? Never done it in your office before?"

"Please tell me I'm having a nightmare and let me wake up," Cole grumbled from her doorway. He scrubbed his eyes before glaring at them. "Can't you two play somewhere else?"

Alex scrambled off Hunter's lap, her face on fire. "Geez. How about a little privacy?" she snapped.

"How about you close your damned door?" he snapped back.

Hunter laughed. "As entertaining as you two are, I need to see Max for a quick minute. I don't think he understands we're serious about our plans." He stood and kissed Alex, then slapped her brother on the back as he passed him. "Later, Cole."

Cole watched him leave, then turned back to her. He helped her pack a few things in boxes—what she'd been doing before Hunter had pulled her into his lap and distracted her. They discussed the kidnapped women, who'd been returned safely to their families. Rebecca had come through with a few emotional scars, but her family and therapist had every assurance of helping her through the hard times.

Peter Omaney had been found dead next to Sarah Moreland's body. The cause of death had been ruled a suicide. Apparently, Sarah had been the key to *his* redemption, and her loss had pushed him over the edge. They'd found Peter's contact at Westlake. But, to everyone's dismay, the man had fled before they could nail him for conspiracy to commit murder.

Every one of the men at Ray's house had been indicted on one charge or another. The bust was a huge coup for Westlake Enterprises, as well as the federal agencies, for taking down Wraith. Max had chosen to remain quiet about their part in the effort, not wanting any undue attention from the government.

"You heard that Thorne, Storm, and Luc are starting work here next week," Cole said as he pocketed a chocolate bar from her desk drawer. The rat. "You still want to leave? I'll miss you."

"Oh, come on. You hated me working here."

"Only because it's dangerous. I liked spending time with you." He drew silent, and the worry in his gaze concerned her.

"Okay, spit it out."

"You and Hunter, are you sure?"

She'd never been more sure about anything in her life. "About running a consulting business with him? Yes. He's wanted to be on his own for a while, and I like the idea of us working on a contractual basis. Between his practical knowledge about security and my business sense and contacts, we'll make a killing. And don't worry, he's as bad as you are about keeping me safe."

"Well, that's one thing, at least." Cole sighed.

"Now, about me loving him? I do. I can't help myself. He's the first guy I've been completely honest with, and he loves me so much." *He just hasn't said it yet, the stubborn man.* But he showed her in so many ways. She smiled, surprised to find tears in her eyes. "I'm so happy with him."

"Aw, Alex. Don't cry." Her brother took her in his arms. "If you like him, I'll like him. I'll *try* to like him," he amended.

She chuckled and wiped her eyes. Cole dropped his arms, and she stepped back, finally on her own in a way she'd never before been. The independence gratified her. "I won't be far, Cole. I mean, I'm living at his place, but we're going to keep an office at the Westlake building. It was the only way Jurek would agree to let Hunter go. I think he wants to keep an eye on us personally."

"Probably." Cole toyed with her stapler. "So you're going to work with him. You love him, and you're living with him. And?"

"And what?"

Hunter answered her, though she hadn't heard him walk down the hall. "*And* he wants to know when we're getting married."

Alex stared at him in shock. They hadn't mentioned marriage. Hell, he still hadn't admitted how he felt about her. She'd stayed with him night and day until he recovered, blathered on and on about how she loved him and worried about him. And then he'd insisted she move in with him. But no talk about a long-term relationship.

"Well?" Cole asked as they stared at one another.

"Answer him, Alex. Are you going to marry me or not?" Hunter demanded. He had the nerve to sound impatient.

"I don't know. No one's *asked* me yet." She glared at him. Good Lord, did she need to spell it out?

Cole smirked, until Hunter said something under his breath. Her brother quickly took his leave.

"What did you say to him?" she asked as Hunter closed the door behind Cole.

"I said if he didn't want to see a repeat of what he'd *seen* before, he'd better get his ass gone."

"Oh." What else could she say to that?

Hunter closed the distance between them. "Marry, me, angel. I want to spend the rest of my life with you."

"That's it?"

He frowned, then dug into his pocket. "Mercenary little thing, aren't you?" He handed her a small box. "Open it."

She did and trembled as she put the square-cut, emerald engagement ring on her finger. "It's beautiful."

"Okay, you're wearing it. That's a yes." Hunter leaned down to kiss her, but she stopped him.

"Hold it. Just *marry me*? What about *I love you*?"

227

"You do? You've never said it before," he teased.

Alex poked him hard in the chest. "I said it about a hundred times while you were in the hospital and since then, you monster. Now tell me. I want to hear you say it." She tried to hold on to her irritation, but the love in his eyes brought only joy.

"I love you, Alexandra Sainte. And I can't live without you. Will you do me the honor of becoming my wife?"

"*Finally.* I love you, too!" She hugged him tight. "I'd love to marry you."

"It's about damn time." He hugged her back and lifted her off the floor. "You're mine, angel. *All mine.*"

About the Author

Marie Harte is an avid reader who loves all things paranormal and futuristic. Reading romances since she was twelve, she fell in love with the warmth of first passion and knew writing was her calling. Twenty-plus years later, the Marine Corps, a foray through Information Technology, a husband and four kids, and her dream has finally come true. Marie lives in Georgia with her family and loves hearing from readers. To read more about Marie, visit www.marieharte.com.

She had no idea what she was looking for
…until it found her.

Bad Karma
© *2010 Theresa Weir*

Officer Daniel Sinclair can spot an outsider a mile away. He ought to know—he's the worst kind. A natural-born native of Egypt, Missouri, who left home and came back citified. Even before he lays eyes on Cleo Tyler, his L.A.-honed suspicions tell him the psychic hired to locate Egypt's missing master key is a fraud. She also possesses a soft, exotic kind of beauty that sets him on edge.

Cleo's used to dealing with skeptics—in fact, she is one. She longs to believe abilities like hers don't exist, yet she can't explain the odd glimpses into other people's lives, nor the terrible flashbacks from her own past. She'd like nothing better than to put on a good show, collect the money, and hit the road. But behind Egypt's quaint façade is a chill she can't shake, and a powerful attraction to Daniel that's stronger than her increasingly desperate need to run.

Cleo more than makes Daniel uncomfortable. She sets him on fire—and sees right through him. And right through the town's charming veneer at something so deadly, her next vision could be her last.

This book has been previously published and revised from its original release.

Warning: Contains explicit sex, explicit fantasies, explicit visions, a to-dream-for alpha hero and a heroine who teaches him to lighten up.

Available now in ebook and print from Samhain Publishing.

A hot chick. A golden blade. Dead bodies.
It's enough to make a cop crazy.

Scythe

© 2009 MK Mancos

Keely Montgomery doesn't spend much time thinking about death. She's too busy working toward a Ph.D. in social work—her ticket out of a low-rent apartment in a New Jersey urban center. Until an angelic courier delivers a scroll from the Office of Death and Dismemberment that could take her career down a new path—as one of Heaven's Holy Assassins.

Her? Become a Scythe? No thanks, not interested. But she underestimates how persistent Heaven can be.

Detective Josiah Adler has seen a lot of weird things during his time on the force. A hot blonde wielding a golden blade, standing over a string of dead bodies? That's a new one. So is the fact that her grisly deeds leave no blood or marks on the bodies.

The woman's effect on his libido is another new development. One that leaves him no choice but to nail her before she kills again. And before his heart no longer stands a chance...

Warning: This book contains wisecracking heavenly bodies, sci-fi geekery and a bulldog named Pugsley.

Available now in ebook from Samhain Publishing.